APPRENTICE OF THE DEAD

The Apprentice Of Anubis

Book 1

LAURA GREENWOOD

A Brief Note

The Egyptian Empire World is set in an alternative universe where the Egyptian Empire never fell and replaced the Roman Empire. The split in the timeline happened after the Ptolemaic dynasty and the final Cleopatra's infamous reign. Instead of Egypt falling into the hands of the Romans, they fought back and gained control of the budding Roman Empire. All religions still exist in the world, but many have been absorbed into the Egyptian religion (this was common practice during their ancient history, so is something I adopted into the series).

For the purposes of this series, the Egyptian Empire spans much of Africa and Europe, as well as some of the Middle East.

I made the decision to keep a lot of the words

and systems we use today (including place names like London and the River Thames) to make the reading experience as smooth as possible. If this was the real progression of events, those things would likely have been named differently.

Things I have kept are the Ancient Egyptian concept of a week (10 days, including a 2 day "weekend"), month (3 weeks), season (4 months) and year (3 seasons plus 5 feast days). The currency they're using is debens (derived from the Ancient Egyptian word for bread - something workers were often paid in). Names have also been influenced by Ancient Egyptian history.

Blurb

Mummification lessons, a new jackal familiar, and temple politics...Ani never expected serving Anubis to be this complicated.

When Ani becomes an apprentice Blessed by Anubis, she finds herself thrown into a world she only ever hoped to be part of.

Between learning how to be an embalmer, being the new owner of a sacred jackal, and a budding rivalry turned friendship with the High Priest's son, Ani has her hands full.

But when she uncovers a plot that could bring the temple to its knees, she has to decide whether to risk her place at the temple or let the injustice slide by unnoticed.

Can she stop the plot before it's too late?

-

Apprentice Of The Dead is book 1 in the

Apprentice Of Anubis, an urban fantasy series based on Egyptian mythology and featuring a slow-burn friends-to-lovers workplace romantic subplot, a jackal familiar, and the duties of an embalmer.

If you love Egyptian mythology, alternative versions of the modern day, temple politics, slow-burn workplace romance, and a world where the gods are real, then start the Apprentice Of Anubis series today with Apprentice Of The Dead.

TEMPLE OF ANUBIS
(LONDON)

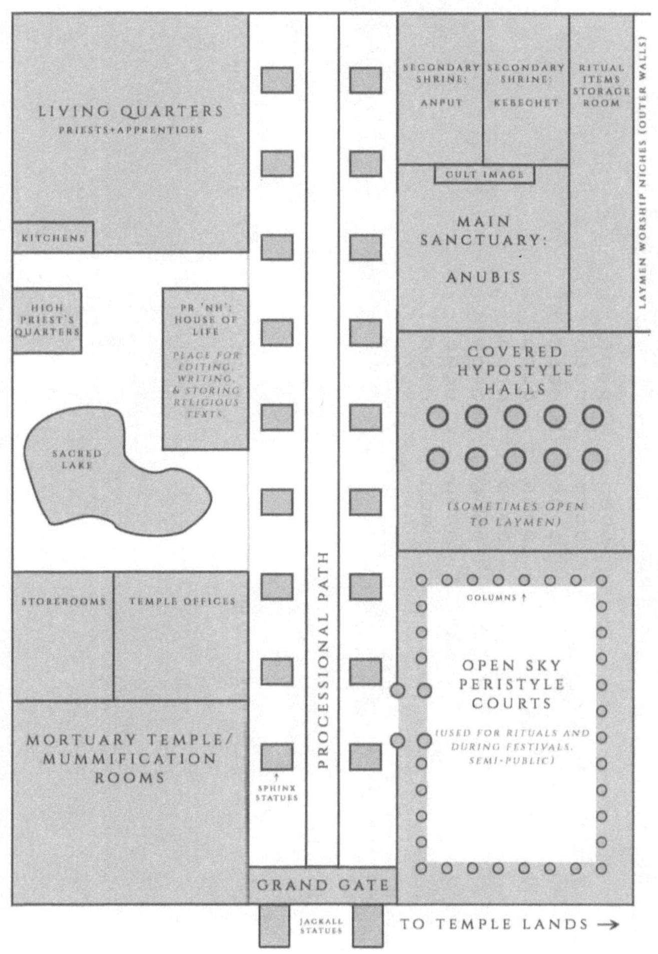

Chapter 1

The primary London Temple of Anubis stands in front of me, with the grand statues of the god flanking the entrance, and stone columns covered in intricate carvings depicting the great journey of gods and mortals alike to the afterlife. Something about it calls to me, just like it does every other time I've passed it, though I've never understood why. Anubis' temple doesn't accept many priestesses, the chance of me ever becoming one of them is small.

"Ani, are you coming?" Nefertiti calls.

I tear my gaze away and turn to my best friend. "Sorry."

"We're going to be late, that's not going to get us a good placement."

More likely it wouldn't get us any. The gods

aren't big fans of tardiness as our teachers have been fond of telling us our entire lives. I'm not sure how they'd know when the gods don't walk among us, they can't tell us what they want. Though I suppose they can influence the world around us. Maybe they'll send one of their legendary plagues down on London just because Neffie and I are late for the Day of Choosing.

She reaches out and grabs my hand, dragging me behind her and down the avenue of temples. Most of the major gods and goddesses have one on this street as it backs onto the Thames and they can move things back and forth using the river.

"I knew we should have gotten the bus," Neffie mutters.

"You hate the bus," I counter.

"But I don't want to be late. You know I want to serve Bastet. How am I going to do that if I'm too late to get a position there?"

"You know they've already chosen who they're going to take, right?" I ask. "They use our school reports..."

"Yes, but not if you're going to be Blessed."

I resist the urge to roll my eyes. "Only some people become Blessed. And not that often by Bastet."

Or Anubis.

Though Neffie has more of a chance of getting what she wants than I do, at least Bastet has chosen a Blessed from the British Isles in the past twenty years. Anubis' jackals are an even rarer sight here than they are everywhere else.

I ignore the thought. There's no point dwelling on whether or not a god is going to choose me to be their priestess. It'll either happen, or it won't. And it's not the end of the world if it doesn't, not all of the current High Priests or Priestesses are Blessed, they rose through the ranks like those before them and now they're some of the most important people in the Egyptian Empire.

Neffie doesn't relax until we've joined a queue of other eighteen-year-olds attending the Day of Choosing. All of us are dressed in our formal wear, which is unfortunate given the light drizzle I can sense in the air. The thin linen shift dresses we're expected to wear aren't particularly practical when it comes to the weather here. But this is what the Pharaoh and his ministers insist we wear for important occasions. They're all warm and cosy in Cairo while those of us in the far reaches of the Empire freeze on days like this.

We shuffle forward, bouncing up and down to

stop ourselves from getting too cold. The line is moving painfully slowly and I just want to get inside.

Nerves flutter in my stomach, though I'm not sure why. This is all decided well in advance. Sometimes, I wish they'd just send us a message rather than making us all line up. But this is the way it's been done for centuries, I doubt they're going to change it now.

"Next," a scribe calls.

The boy in front of us approaches the desk.

"Do you want to go first?" Neffie asks, a hint of nervousness in her voice.

At least I'm not alone, though that isn't surprising. This has been all she can talk about for weeks.

"Next."

"Good luck," Neffie says, pushing me forward.

I want to protest and say she should go first, but it's too late. The scribe is already there waiting for me to tell him my name. His stylus is poised over the screen of his tablet and I doubt he'll be happy with anyone wasting his time.

"Ankhesenamun, from Seshat Secondary School, London." To my surprise, my voice doesn't even shake.

He taps on the screen, but I can't see what he's

writing. He holds the tablet up and glances between me and the information on the screen.

He nods and gestures for me to continue inside.

I walk slowly to give Neffie a chance to catch up. The jangle of her bracelets is a welcome sound, and she's soon linking her arm through mine.

Blissfully, the main courtyard has a roof covering it. No doubt they tried to have it be open-air, but decided against it when they realised how much it rains here.

Hundreds of eighteen-year-olds mill around and a low murmur fills the room from their chatter. Unsurprisingly, most people are standing with their friends and not using the opportunity to get to know some of the other attendees. Throughout the Empire, there will be gatherings like this of eighteen-year-olds hoping to gain employment in one of the various temples. We're just two of them.

"What if I don't get to serve Bastet?" Neffie whispers.

"You will," I promise, though I have no idea if that's actually true. It seems unlikely they won't take her when she's been at the top of the class for three years running.

She grimaces, clearly not so sure about that.

I reach out and pat her arm. I wish I could do

more, but honestly, I'm terrified myself. I've never felt a strong connection to any of the gods other than Anubis. I don't know what's going to happen at the end of the day when I'm assigned to serve one.

At least it's not a life sentence. I can drop out of the apprentice program at any point, but even that comes with complications. Not from the temples, obviously, but my parents are another matter. Mum has wanted nothing other than for me to enter priestesshood since I was old enough to walk.

A gong sounds, reverberating around the room and causing everyone to fall silent.

Without anyone saying a word, we all file into neat lines, standing too far away from one another to touch.

I hold my head up high and bunch my hands into fists, trying not to let my concerns show on my face. This is an official function, it won't be a good thing if I show how uncomfortable I am by it all.

Grand doors at the front of the room creak as they open up onto the raised dais at the front. They're flanked by ornate pillars carved and painted with all of the major gods, and several of the smaller ones too, a demonstration that this place is shared by all of them. The High Priests and

Priestesses of London file onto the raised stage, draped in the finest linen and dripping with the best gold and jewels money can buy. Prestige isn't the only advantage of being the leader of a priesthood.

Despite the sheer number of people in the room, it's almost silent. Unnervingly so. But we're all waiting for the High Priest of Amun to step forward and officially open the ceremony. It's rare for him to be away from the Canterbury temple, but this is definitely classed as a special occasion.

I scan the line of officials on the stage, trying to pinpoint which of the group he is. I've only ever seen him from a distance, and when everyone is dressed up the way they currently are, it's hard to tell them apart. If I was closer, I was sure I'd be able to see the various different animals and symbols decorating their jewels that would let me know.

A man close to the middle steps forward and opens his arms wide. "Good morning, all. Welcome to the Day of Choosing. May the gods in their infinite wisdom choose those who will serve them honourably and well."

Several of the priests on stage nod along with him.

"Let us commence the ceremony for the Blessed." He gestures to the side.

A smaller door opens, and through it comes a small black cat. She winds her way through the students, sniffing and trying to decide which of them she likes the most. Naysayers like to say the Blessed part of the ceremony is completely made up. It isn't the gods guiding the choices of the animals, it's all coincidence.

I'm not sure what to believe. The gods are real, there's no doubt in my mind about that. But I doubt they care very much about the ways of mortals. Especially not teenage ones who are prone to change their minds about things.

Around the room, several other cats make their way through the lines.

Neffie sucks in a deep breath as the cat passes her. I know she's hoping it will stop in front of her and she'll be Bastet's Blessed. It's the only way of changing the minds of the priests and priestesses. Otherwise, we end up at the places we've already been assigned, even if we're not aware of them.

Unsurprisingly, the cat passes Neffie by and heads back to the room it came from without choosing anyone. I've heard rumours this is what happens most of the time. The animals come out, walk around, and then go back to where they came from.

If they appear at all.

It's been a couple of years since one of Anubis' jackals has even made an appearance, and that was in a different country.

The process repeats with a few different creatures, including a cold looking ibis and a gangly deer.

At least we're only made to do this with some animals. Gods and goddesses with more dangerous sacred animals tend to show their feelings in other, safer, ways. Which I'm glad of. I don't like the idea of having a crocodile creeping between us to try and inform us of Sobek's will.

A soft murmur comes from the front of the hall.

"Ani, look," Neffie whispers, pointing to the front.

She needn't have bothered. My gaze is already fixated on the black form leaving the door and making its way amongst the assembled potential priests.

One of Anubis' jackals has made itself known.

Despite knowing how unlikely it is the god will choose me, I hold my breath, counting down the minutes until it passes and I know I'm not the only one. I've done everything I can to make it possible, including taking the right classes and focusing on anatomy and the natural sciences at school, but I have to be realistic and accept that the chances of serving Anubis are slim. In all likelihood, I'll leave here as a trainee priestess for Isis, *just* like Mum wants.

To my surprise, the jackal appears in front of me and sits down. It cocks its head to the side, a funny look on its face. I don't know if it's male or female, but I do know that it's come for me.

Hundreds of eyes are on me. Which isn't enough to dissuade me from reaching out my hand and gently brushing it against the jackal's head.

Its eyes close, as if enjoying the scratches.

A man steps forward to join the High Priest of Amun and clears his throat. "Anubis has spoken. His sacred jackal, Matia, has made her choice."

That answers that one. The jackal is female. Somehow that feels right.

Another priest makes his way through the crowd towards me. "What's your name?" he asks.

"Ankhesenamun, but people call me Ani." My voice shakes ever so slightly, but I put that down to the amount of pressure there is from the various people watching.

He notes something down on his tablet. "Please make your way through the doors over there." He points to the left. "High Priest Ahmose will take you through everything you need to know."

I nod, not knowing what else I can possibly do.

Slowly, I turn and make my way to the doors, only noticing after a few steps that Matia is following me.

I wish I could tell Neffie that I'll message her later. But we've been friends long enough for me to be confident knowing she doesn't think I've abandoned her.

And that she'll want to hear everything about my conversation with the High Priest of Anubis.

Chapter 2

The room is smaller than I expect it to be, but beautiful nonetheless. There are ornate paintings on all of the walls which include far more detail than I'd expect from a room that's only used once a year.

I resist the urge to pace while I wait for the High Priest.

Matia has trotted in behind me and is still looking at me with an intrigued expression. There's something about the jackal that's both majestic and a little funny looking. But she seems good-natured, and I suppose that's what matters.

"Hello," I say to her.

She cocks her head to the side as if to return the greeting.

Do jackals normally make a noise? I have to

admit to not being sure, she's the first one I've seen up close.

"Do you want more scratches?" I ask.

I take her stillness for assent and reach out to ruffle the top of her head. She makes a soft rumbling sound that I take to mean enjoyment.

Footsteps echo from down the corridor and I pull back, standing up straight so I look smart when I'm faced with High Priest Ahmose for the first time. I know enough about being Blessed to know it effectively makes him my boss, and I don't want to get off on the wrong foot.

Once he's in the room with me, it only takes a moment for me to realise how he became the High Priest. There's something about the way he holds himself and the air around him that just says authority.

I stand even straighter, which is surprising when I didn't even realise it was possible.

"Good morning, Ankhesenamun," he says.

"Good morning, High Priest." I dip my head as a sign of respect.

"I will admit that I wasn't expecting a Blessed for our temple today." He doesn't seem annoyed by it, just intrigued.

"I wasn't expecting to be Blessed either," I

counter. Though there was a small part of me that hoped I'd be able to enter the Temple of Anubis, I didn't really think it would happen.

There's still a voice in my head telling me that this isn't real and there's been a mistake. The High Priest is only here to tell me to go back to the hall and wait to be assigned to my real temple.

"But I'm not one to turn down Anubis' gifts. Are you?" he asks.

I shake my head. "Absolutely not."

"Good. Then you'll be expected to report to the temple on the first day of next week. I'll arrange for supplies for Matia to be delivered to your residence for the days until then, and for your room at the temple to have space for her..."

"I'm taking Matia home with me?" I can't keep the surprise out of my voice.

She must know we're talking about her, as she pushes her head against my hand as if asking for more scratches.

"Of course. She is a blessing from the gods and is a sign of your connection to Anubis."

"Oh."

"She also seems to have taken a shine to you." A small smile lifts the corners of his lips, but it's gone a moment later, almost as if he doesn't want me to see it.

"It seems so." Is that a good thing?

"I look forward to seeing what you achieve once you're our apprentice," he says, turning on his heels in a clear signal that the conversation is over.

"I'm sorry, High Priest," I call out. "But what am I supposed to do now? No one's told me."

"You can do whatever you want," Ahmose responds. "Until the new week, your time is your own. You can wait for your friends to finish the ceremony and celebrate with them, or you can return home. The choice is yours."

Oh. That's somewhat anticlimactic.

The High Priest leaves me alone with my new jackal. I look down at her, but only get a quizzical expression in response. I'm sure I'll learn more about her facial cues as I get to know her better, but for now, Matia is a mystery to me.

I glance around the room to see if there's a lead or something similar for Matia. I'm not sure whether I need to have her on one, or how wild she's going to be. So far, she's seemed fairly docile, but I'm not sure if that'll last.

Unfortunately, there doesn't seem to be anything.

"You're just going to have to behave," I tell her.

She makes a soft yipping sound. It's almost like agreement, but it really is impossible to tell.

"We're going to go outside and wait for my friend to finish with the ceremony," I say. "After that, we'll go home." And break it to Mum that I'm not going to be serving Isis.

The corridors are deserted, no doubt everyone is still in the hall, unless there's been another Blessed, but it's impossible to know without being inside the room. Hopefully, Neffie will be done soon so she can fill me in.

Matia trots along beside me, seemingly happy to follow. It's going to make things easier if she behaves this way.

The moment the cold air hits me, I remember I don't have a coat and it's probably a terrible idea to be outside without one. But it's too late. Especially as I've been told I need to leave.

I glance at the temple door, wondering whether I should leave Neffie to it and just go home, but I push the thought aside fairly quickly. She'll kill me if we leave without filling one another in on everything that's gone on. And I'm sure she'll want to meet Matia.

As if by instinct, I reach down and scratch behind the jackal's ears. She pushes her head against my hand, urging me to do it more. It feels so natural to be like this with her, which is odd as I've never had a pet before. I guess that's going to change now.

Excited voices sound from the temple, making me stand bolt-upright. I don't want to be caught slouching by the wrong person.

A crowd of teenagers streams through the door. I scan their faces, searching for my best friend. Many of the others appear to be excited, but there are some people who seem as if they're heartbroken, and others who seem more bored than anything else.

It's an interesting mix.

"Ani!" a familiar voice shouts.

I turn to find Neffie running towards me, her hand tightly gripped against the linen of her skirt so she can hurry over to me. She throws her arms around me and I hug her back, laughing ever so slightly. I don't even need to ask to know that she's been assigned to serve Bastet. If she hadn't, she'd be in absolute tears right now.

"Good news?" I ask as she pulls away from me, just to be sure I've read the situation right.

She nods eagerly. "You're looking at one of the newest apprentice priestesses of Bastet."

"Congratulations." I grin widely. This has been her dream for so long, I'm glad she gets to live it.

"Thank you."

"What happened after I left?" I ask, my curiosity getting the better of me. I'm never going to attend another Day of Choosing again, this is it for me. For all of us. And I missed the main part of it.

"Nothing really interesting," she admitted. "A few more Blessed, but none as surprising as you."

I nod. It isn't unexpected, there are so many gods, and most of them choose their Blessed this way.

"And then they made us line up and gave each of us a scroll with our assignment in it." She lifts her left hand, and sure enough, she's holding one. I glance past her at the others and notice most of them are holding one too. "But that's not what I want to be talking about. I need to know what happened to you. Are you going to serve Anubis?"

"Yes."

She squeaks and jumps up and down on the spot. "You've always wanted that."

"I haven't." I glance away so she can't tell I'm lying.

"Pfft. Please. I have eyes, Ani. I see how you look at the temple every time you pass."

"Okay, fine. It is what I wanted."

"I knew it." A smug note enters her voice. "And the jackal?" She looks past me to where my new companion is waiting surprisingly calmly.

"Is now my responsibility. She's called Matia."

"Hello." She reaches out a hand.

The jackal watches her warily before trotting forward and pushing her head into Neffie's hand.

"She seems to like me," Neffie says.

"As far as I can tell, she's friendly to everyone." Though considering how few people I've come across so far, it's hard to know for sure. "But I know nothing about keeping sacred animals."

"I guess it's time to learn," she responds. "I expect to get lots of messages about her antics."

A soft laugh escapes me. "Do you really think I'd deny you them?"

"Not at all. But that can wait until tomorrow. We should go out and celebrate."

"Yes, we should," I agree. "What did you have in mind?"

"We could head to the wine bar we've been meaning to go to?" she suggests.

"Oh, that's a great idea." We've been meaning to go for a while, but never seem to have the time.

"Then that's settled." She slips her arm through mine. "Will Matia just follow?"

I shrug. "As far as I know." I guess we'll see what happens. I wish they'd given me more guidance on what to do with her, especially when she's a sacred animal straight from the temple of Anubis.

We set off, both of us full of excitement about the start to our careers. I feel like the whole world is open to us now.

"We need to go via my house though, I don't have any money on me," I say.

She groans. "I wish they'd let us bring a handful of debens with us, it'd make everything so much easier."

"Even lockers to put a bag in would help."

"True. If we're going via your house, I want to raid your wardrobe for some comfier clothes. I hate this." She gestures to her dress.

"You know you're going to have to wear this kind of thing more once you're a priestess?"

Neffie groans. "Even more reason to make the most of the time I have left where I don't have to. You're lucky you'll get to wear comfortable clothes."

"Only while up to my neck in dead bodies. I'll

still be wearing dresses for formal occasions." I think. There aren't many priestesses of Anubis to base my knowledge on. And none of them are in London.

"Hmm. True. I'll take the formal wear over dead people any day."

"And that's why you're more suited to Bastet than Anubis. But we should get a move on or everyone else is going to drink all the wine before we get there."

For the first time in weeks, I feel light and hopeful. I don't think I realised how much the upcoming Day of Choosing was affecting me. But now it's over and we get to enjoy our last few days of freedom before starting our training. And I'm going to make the most of it.

Chapter 3

Matia trots along beside me as I make my way to the entrance of the temple. Huge statues of Anubis tower above each side of the gate, making it obvious to everyone who is worshipped within.

After years of simply staring at them whenever I walk past, I finally get a chance to find out what the inside looks like.

Excitement and nerves war for dominance inside me. Being Blessed gets me here, but that's it. Being the only priestess in a temple full of priests is going to be hard. At least with Matia by my side, I don't have to do it alone.

I clutch my bag tightly, trying not to think about how much can go wrong. It's weird not to have much with me, but my day-to-day clothing will be provided by the temple, and I won't have much space so have only brought a few of my belongings from home. The rest will stay in my childhood room until I move up the ranks and gain more space in my living quarters. Or something like that.

A straight ceremonial path stretches from the entrance to the back wall and a smaller gate which leads to the Thames and Anubis Quay. Sphinxes flank each side of the path, with a few barque stations dotted alongside them for when the priests need to rest during their processionals.

Priests and civilian workers for the temple are already going about their day, some of them are hurrying to other parts of the temple, and others are carrying heavy-looking boxes.

Thankfully, the sun has decided to make an appearance today, so I don't have to battle with that as well as trying to find the living quarters. The information sent over along with a few days worth of supplies for Matia told me to head towards the back of the temple, but considering how big the grounds are, that's not actually much help.

I take a deep breath and continue down the path. I scan each of the buildings as I pass, grateful to discover that some of them are at least labelled with what they are. I suspect I'm going to be spending a lot of time in the mortuary near the front of the complex.

Matia brushes against my legs, eager to be as close to me as possible. I never thought I'd be able to forge a bond with an animal as deeply and quickly as I have with her, and I'm glad to have her company as I continue on this new part of my life. Though a small part of me wishes Neffie could be here instead of at the temple of Bastet. But that's not fair of me. She's wanted this for so long, I wouldn't want to actually take it from her just so I can be more comfortable.

I finally arrive at the building at the back of the compound. I pause for a moment, taking it in.

My new home.

It's plainer than the rest of the temple but is still a masterpiece of architecture and decoration.

I take a deep breath.

"This is it," I say to Matia, reaching down to pat her head. "We're going to be spending a lot of time here, I hope you like it."

I wonder how it compares to where she used to live. Considering she's a sacred jackal, there's a good chance she's taking a step down by coming to live with me.

No wonder she likes sleeping on the bed.

I step through the entrance to find a portly priest with a tablet standing in the entrance hall.

"Ankhesenamun?" he asks.

"That's me." I don't worry about how he knows who I am. Considering I'm going to be the only female apprentice, it's fairly easy to work out.

"You're in room sixty-four. You need to go up the stairs and to the left. Here's your key." He hands it to me.

"Thanks." I slip it into my pocket.

"You're expected in the mortuary in two hours. Your jackal isn't to attend," he continues.

It makes sense. As much as it's a comfort to have Matia by my side, she's still an animal, I'm sure some of the fresher bodies probably smell good to her.

"Is there anything else I need to know?" I ask the priest.

"It'll all be covered in your briefing this after-noon," he responds. "So long as you attend that, you'll be fine." He flashes me a smile that seems genuine.

"Thank you." I turn and head towards the stairs, taking them two at a time.

Matia bounces up alongside me, with far more energy than I think I've ever had. Maybe one day I'll learn how she gets it so I can replicate it.

I count down the doors until I come to the one with sixty-four written on it.

I take a deep breath and slip the key into the lock. I have no idea what to expect on the inside.

The room is smaller than the one I have at home, but not by much. A medium-sized bed is pushed against the wall. It's just about big enough for the two of us.

Other than that, there's just the standard furniture. A large desk and an open wardrobe full of the standard attire for priests in the mortuary. I should make sure to hang up my formal dresses in there before they get too wrinkled in my bag.

A simple black outfit is lying on the bed, which I assume is what I'm supposed to wear for the briefing.

Matia trots inside and heads straight under the desk, sniffing loudly. That must be where her food is.

I sit on the bed and stare at the wall, disbelief flooding through me. Despite the odds, I've actually managed to find myself in the temple belonging to Anubis. So long as I complete my training, I'm going to be one of his few priestesses. I know I shouldn't let that get to my head, but it's a little hard when everything is coming up in my favour.

But despite that, I know it's going to take everything I have to keep up and do well.

Something I'm determined to do.

Chapter 4

I step inside the mortuary, my eyes widening at the incredible stench. I'm not sure what I expected, but it isn't this.

None of the trainee priests are responding to it, so I stand up tall and pretend it's not bothering me. I suspect it's something I'll get used to the more time I spend around dead bodies.

Maybe I should have gone into service for Isis after all. I doubt that would have involved dead people. But I know that's wrong. Not just because Anubis chose me, but because I've been working for this for years. I want to serve the dead, to help them through the process that means they can travel to the afterlife. The first time someone talked about it as a career, I knew it was exactly what I wanted to do.

A balding priest steps into the room with a scribe trailing along behind him. I'm not sure what he's here for, but I imagine I'm going to find out.

The priest clears his throat. "Good morning, welcome to your first day as apprentices. Aren't there supposed to be ten of you?"

I glance around at my fellow students, counting their heads. Hmm. He's right, there is someone missing.

"Never mind. By the time you become full priests, there won't be anyway." The man's gaze lingers on me, as if to make a point about me not belonging here.

It's hard to ignore it. He's not wrong. There are only twenty priestesses of Anubis throughout the entire world, none of them are very high in the command structures, and most of them are from countries with smaller populations where they end up needing to take women in order to deal with the number of dead produced. Some of the other priesthoods can be pickier, but no matter how many priests Anubis has, the dead keep on coming.

"You'll be spending your first few months in here. You'll learn to process the dead as they arrive and to perform the most basic funerary rites," the priest announces.

"Does that mean we won't be making mummies?" a red-haired guy asks from the back.

"Absolutely not. The traditional rites are reserved for the most elite visitors to the temple. They are carried out by highly trained professionals, of which you are not." The expression on the man's face says it all. He's not impressed that one of the new apprentices thinks they have what it takes to perform proper mummification.

"So, what will we be doing?" the boy to the left of me asks. He can't possibly be eighteen with the baby face he's sporting.

"At first, you'll be cleaning the embalming room and doing what the priests tell you. Then, you'll move on to embalming sacred animals and donated bodies..."

I raise an eyebrow. Donated? I wonder if they know what's going to happen to them.

The priest doesn't hear my silent question, which isn't a surprise. No one can read minds.

"Once you have proved yourselves capable of the basics, you will move on to processing the bodies of those who have donated organs and other tissues in order to pay for their mummification, as well as dealing with those who choose natural mummification as an option," he continues.

That's interesting. Mum has always talked about wanting a natural one, but I thought it was going to be hard to achieve given that we don't live anywhere near the desert. But if they're offering it at the temple, then there must be a way to do it.

I can't wait to tell her.

"All right, this is Hori," he says, gesturing for a younger man who barely looks ten years older than us. "He'll be your supervisor while you're working in this part of the temple."

"Thank you." Hori steps in front of us and scans the nine of us.

Before he can say anything else, the door clatters open and a guy I don't recognise saunters in and comes to join us without a word of an apology.

"You're late," Hori says.

"I had a meeting with my father," the new apprentice replies, more than a small hint of arrogance in his tone. "You might know him, High Priest Ahmose."

Collective groans come from my fellow students. I simply glare at the newcomer. No wonder he's an arrogant ass if he's the son of the High Priest. That shouldn't get him any special treatment in my scroll, but I don't think that's how it's going to work in reality. No one ever said the temples were nepotism free.

"Don't be late again," Hori responds without seeming the slightest bit impressed. I like him already. "Being part of the priesthood is hard work. If you don't want that, then you'd better leave now."

Unsurprisingly, no one moves.

"Very well. My notes say that one of you is Blessed. Who is it?" His gaze flits right over me and lands on the High Priest's son.

I clear my throat. "That's me."

Suddenly, I'm the centre of attention. Even more so than I was on the Day of Choosing when my jackal walked up to me. I miss her companionship already, but unsurprisingly, I'm not allowed to bring a scavenger into a place filled with dead bodies, so she's safely back in my room doing whatever jackals do when they're alone.

In Hori's defence, he barely skips a beat after learning I'm the one Anubis chose. "Don't expect any special treatment because of it. Being Blessed may have gotten you into the temple, but it doesn't change anything now you're here. That goes for the rest of you too. I expect everyone to put in the work, or you'll find yourselves back in your parents' homes before the end of the day. Does anyone have a problem with that?"

We all mutter agreement. I certainly have every intention of working as hard as I can. I know it's going to be harder for me. Not just because I'm female, but also because I'm Blessed. I know it's going to mean I'm scrutinised more and every success will be put down to Anubis' favour, while every mistake will throw up the question of why he picked me.

I try not to think about it. I can either drive myself crazy trying to meet everyone's expectations, or I can focus on trying my best and learning as much as I can. I know which of the two is going to get the biggest result.

"If you follow me, I'll take you on a tour of the mortuary," Hori says, gesturing further inside the building.

The High Priest's son barges his way to the front, with the rest of us following behind. Maybe if I get nervous about proving myself, I should focus my efforts on making sure he isn't at the top of the class.

"We're going to start with the easiest on the stomach," Hori says with a slight smile. "These are the storerooms. While you're in the first part of your training, you'll probably find yourselves in here a lot."

We follow him into a huge room filled with containers.

"What's inside them?" one of the others asks.

Hori heads towards the closest one and pushes the lid off. Small figurines of a mummified Osiris, complete with crossed arms holding a miniature crook and flail, sit within, each well-carved but identical.

"These are amulets placed on the body during the embalming process. Which figurines and the number given depend on what package the family has ordered," Hori says. "You'll each have to learn what and where the amulets are. You'll each be expected to study the introductory packs being delivered to your rooms tonight so you have some idea of what each of them is for."

"Father says we were the first temple in Europe to start mass manufacture of amulets and statuettes for funeral purposes," the High Priest's son says.

The expression on Hori's face says just how little he thinks of him. "Nikare is right. Though there were many temples that made these items in bulk, we are one of the first to switch the process over to mass manufacture. It means that we can offer more to the less advantaged clients and give them the burial they desire. Not all of our clients buy these from us. Despite them being the cheapest option on the market, some people prefer the personal touch and will either make amulets themselves or will commission a craftsman to do it."

One of the apprentices raises their hand.

"Yes..." Hori trails off, expecting him to supply his name.

"Djou."

"What's your question, Djou?" Hori asks.

"Why do we allow them to do that? Isn't it better for the temple profits if we sell them the whole package including the amulets and figurines?" Djou wrings his hands together as if already regretting saying anything.

"That's an excellent question. While we do need to make a profit in order to sustain the temple, our first duty is to serve Anubis and that means preparing people for the afterlife in the way they want. We should always respect the wishes of those who have passed and their families."

Hori's words strike deeply within me. I think they're one of the reasons I've always felt so drawn to this place. People die. No matter how rich they are, or how loved, there's no escaping the end. But then we all have a chance of making it to Duat, passing through into the next life where everyone we love will be waiting. It's a comforting thought, and one I've always felt keenly within my soul.

"All right, on to the next room," he announces.

"Are the books of the dead in here too?" the ginger boy asks.

"No, they're kept in the House of Life, you'll have passed it on your way here along with the sacred lake."

Ah. That's what the building is.

"Why are they in a different place?"

Hori smiles. He seems impressed by the questions so far. "It's partly due to tradition, and partly because of the skills needed. The scribes wouldn't be any good at the embalming process, and the embalmers wouldn't know where to start when it came to sacred text preparation. By keeping the two disciplines separate, everyone can focus on what's important."

I imagine the scribes not liking the smell of the mortuary is also part of it. I hope we don't have to deal with a lot of visitors because it is not nice.

We file after Hori as he points out the features of the rest of the building. The offices aren't particularly interesting, with a similar layout to just about every other office I've ever seen.

But the mummification rooms are different. Hori doesn't show us the more specialised ones. I assume we have to work our way up to those ones.

The main room stretches the entire length of the building, with close to a hundred workbenches. Not all of them have a body on them, but I imagine there are times when they do. Priests run back and forth dealing with things I don't yet understand.

"You'll be spending the first part of your training in this room," Hori says, gesturing around.

The apprentice I now know as Djou turns a slight shade of grey as he studies the scene in front of us. I'm not sure if it's the smell, the sight of one of the priests with his hands in a man's stomach, or the bloodstains littering the floor, but something isn't sitting well with him.

"If you want to step outside, I'll cover for you," I whisper.

He flashes me an uneasy smile. "Thanks, but I'll be okay."

I nod, not wanting to push it any further. At least he knows my offer is there. I turn my attention back to Hori who is still talking about his expectations for the ten of us.

"You'll be doing odd tasks that the priests assign to you, whether that's clearing the floor, disposing of unwanted debris, or fetching amulets. Once you're cleared to start working on the bodies themselves, you'll be transferred to one of the smaller rooms where you'll work on animals, and later on humans. The process is going to be strenuous. We do not allow tardiness and you are expected to put in the work needed. No matter who you are, or how you got here."

Nikare looks over his shoulder and grins at me, as if assuming Hori is talking about me with that statement. But from the expression on our supervisor's face and the direction he's looking in, I suspect the words were aimed at Nikare himself.

It doesn't matter what he thinks. I'm going to prove I'm worthy of my position to everyone here.

Chapter 5

I check my phone to confirm Neffie's instructions as I make my way through the warren of Bastet's temple. Even though I know I'm allowed into this part of it, I worry about being told off for being here. But it's my day off and I'm finally getting to spend some time with my best friend after a month of late nights and hard work. I've had rest days already, two every week like everyone else. But until now, they haven't matched up with Neffie's.

I finally find her door and knock a few times.

"Come in," she calls.

I push on it, holding it open so Matia can come through. I don't think I'm the only one who is glad to have time away from the temple.

"Ani!" My best friend jumps to her feet and throws her arms around me.

"Weren't you expecting me?" I ask.

"Yes. But I missed you even more than I thought I did." She pulls away and gestures for the two of us to sit on her bed.

"I get it," I promise. And I do. Seeing her is reassuring. I've missed seeing her every day.

I scan her room, unsurprised to find it similar to mine. I imagine most of the apprentices in the city have the same kind of rooms. Except for Nikare. He talks about how much space he has in his father's house all the time.

"How are you?" I ask. "Is it everything you wanted it to be?"

From what I can see, life in Bastet's temple is agreeing with her. She's glowing, and not in a magical way.

"It is," she responds pushing her hand through her bouncy brown curls. "Everyone is so nice. But no matter what I tell them, they all use my full name." It's impossible to miss the frustration in her voice, but maybe that's because I know it's there.

"Your name is pretty," I point out.

"So is yours. But I bet they're not all calling you Ankhesenamun at every turn."

"They're not," I agree. "But that's because I'm in a temple full of men. It's different for you."

"It'd be different if I wasn't named after the queen of a heretic." She grimaces, her distaste radiating from it.

She has a point. Nefertiti isn't a name I'd choose for myself either. It's pretty, but there are certain connotations it brings up. Even after thousands of years.

"You're not supposed to refer to Akhenaten or Nefertiti as heretics anymore," I point out.

She sighs and drops onto her bed. "I know we're not. But that doesn't change anything, does it? I'm still named after someone who believes there's only one god. If I'd entered Akhenaten's temple, then people would understand. But here..."

"It's been over three thousand years. People have forgotten who they even were."

Neffie snorts. "Except that they made a big song and dance about accepting Aten a few centuries back. People can go to temple and worship him as the only god in existence, even though they have plenty of proof that's not the case."

I shrug. "People can worship whoever they want to."

"Aren't you supposed to say everyone should worship Anubis?" She raises an eyebrow.

A soft chuckle escapes me. "The world would be a very boring place if everyone wanted to serve the same god. I'd rather stick with the variety."

"You're very hard to argue with, Ani."

"That's part of my charm," I joke.

"Hmm. That may be, but it isn't solving the problem of what to do about people using my name."

"You can ask them to call you something else?" I suggest. "People have renaming ceremonies all the time when they think they've found something that suits them better. If you chose something to do with Bastet, people would understand and think you were doing something great."

Neffie sighs. "Can you imagine Mum's face if I told her I was changing my name? She'd have a stroke."

Ah, yes, that is a bit of a problem. I don't imagine her parents being particularly pleased about that. They took a long time to come around to her friends calling her Neffie.

"At least she didn't call you Cleopatra?"

"Eurgh. Can you imagine? There are so many people called that."

"I thought you'd have more of a problem being associated with that time in history." Cleopatra may be a common name, but a lot of people still try to avoid anything to do with the Ptolemaic dynasty, blaming them for the erosion of Egyptian identity and making way for the war with the Roman Empire. I don't see what the problem is when the Egyptian Empire is the one that won the war, but people can be a little strange.

"I'm named after a heretic," she reminds me. "Being named after a Pharaoh that history doesn't like might actually be preferable."

"Has anyone said anything to you about it?"

Neffie has always disliked her name, but it seems to have reached new levels.

"Only this boy."

I raise an eyebrow. "Tell me more."

"There's nothing to tell," she responds, far too quickly for me to believe her.

"Want to try again?" A soft grunt escapes me as I reposition and sit up on the bed.

Neffie sighs dramatically. "He's one of the initiates of Ptah we practise with for official ceremonies. He thinks my name is a joke."

"Then you should make sure you trip him by accident during training." I wiggle my eyebrows.

Matia approaches the bed, having finished her appraisal of the room. Before I can say anything, Neffie pats the covers and the jackal jumps up, curling into a tight ball and going to sleep. It seems she feels safe here.

"Really, Ani? Is that what you've been doing when the other apprentices tease you?"

I shrug. "I don't need to. They're all too scared of Anubis' wrath."

"How could I forget you're Blessed by a god," she mutters.

"It's not that much of an advantage," I admit. "Mostly people just completely ignore it. They're too wrapped up in the son of the High Priest who started his training at the same time as us."

"Don't tell me he's getting preferential treatment?" She sounds outraged at the possibility.

"Oh, he's not. Our supervisor seems to be done with him already. I think they'd kick him out if he wasn't any good. But he works hard even if he does grandstand constantly."

"You almost sound like you admire him."

I give out a sharp laugh. Me, admire Nikare? Hardly. "Only when he's not around to annoy me," I mutter.

"Mmhmm."

"No, seriously. When I don't have to deal with him, I can see that he's smart and good at what we do. But then he starts talking and I just want to punch him." That may be a bit of an understatement.

"Ah, one of those."

"Yep. But I know it's better not to say anything about it." I scratch Matia's head absentmindedly. "Everyone might be determined to treat him the same as the rest of us, but I know that doesn't really mean anything. His father is still my boss."

"I can see how that's a bit of a problem. Are you at least getting to do interesting things?"

I nod. "We've already moved on to embalming animals. I thought it would take longer."

"Maybe they're prepping you because of the vizier?"

I frown, wondering what she's talking about. "What about him?"

"Haven't you heard? He's sick."

"But I thought he was one of the youngest viziers ever?" I remember him being elected and the controversy surrounding it.

"He is, but there have been whispers going around that he's very sick. He's been spotted visiting the temples of Heka, Isis, and Serket."

My eyebrows knit together. "Could it be someone in his family?" The combination of temples does suggest that he's sick, they're where most of the best doctors are stationed.

"No idea. I've never seen him going into one of the temples, but the older priestesses like to gossip and don't think about who can overhear them."

"That doesn't seem like the smartest thing to do."

She shrugs. "Maybe not, but I don't think that's going to stop them."

Footsteps sound from the corridor outside Neffie's room. Matia lifts her head up and lets out a sound similar to a growl.

"Rest," I command.

She whines and sets her head back down on her paws.

"Good girl."

"You seem to have bonded well," Neffie says.

I nod. "I don't know if it's the magic of her choosing me, or if we just happen to click, but she's so easy to get along with so long as she doesn't make a mess in my room while I'm gone."

Neffie wrinkles her nose. "Does that happen often?"

"More than I'd like. The long days are hard on

her, but when I get caught up in my duties, there's nothing I can do about it." I try to repress the guilt welling up within me.

"You'll just have to work your way up into the hierarchy so you can keep her with you."

"I don't know if that can happen if I stay in the mortuary. The dead smell too good to her."

Distaste crosses her features. "You need to work on how you tell people that."

"Sorry, I've become a bit desensitised to it all." Being around dead bodies all day, even just the animals, makes me see death in a way I never have before. There's something peaceful about being able to help prepare the person or creature for their journey to the afterlife. But the shock is definitely gone. The dead are just that.

"It's weird to think about you doing that all day," she admits. "We don't see death nearly as often as we used to anymore."

"True." Coffins are normally sealed at funerals too, and even if they aren't, it's almost impossible to get a good look at the person within. "Maybe it would help people understand if they saw more of the process, but I doubt that's ever going to happen."

"Ah, you mean the temple of Anubis doesn't want to share its secrets?" she teases.

"They haven't even shared their secrets with us yet, so I doubt they'd be willing to let the general public in on them."

"That's a shame. I think I'd take some comfort in knowing what will happen to my body after I die," she muses.

"Wouldn't it be better to focus on what happens to your soul instead?"

"Not really. I already know the answer to that. I'll travel to the Hall of Judgement and have my heart weighed and then go on the Lake of Lilies. You know how it goes."

"I do." Everyone does, it's one of the most commonly shared images no matter what the building is for. All of the gods have a purpose when it comes to the afterlife, even if it's a small one. It leads to a lot of paintings and statues around the subject matter, but not a lot of conversations about the body side of things.

"You'll tell me when you learn, right?" she asks. "Even if it is against the rules?"

A soft chuckle escapes me. "Everyone knows *keep this a secret* doesn't include best friends."

Neffie's laughter joins my own. "Very true. And

I give you full permission to rant about this Nikare guy as much as you want, it sounds like you're going to need it." She shoots me a knowing look.

"I'm sorry, I can't help it. There's just something about him."

"It's fine. Sometimes it happens. You're just in the unfortunate position of not actually being able to get away from him."

I groan. "Tell me about it."

"Is there a chance you're annoyed by him because he's better than you?"

I resist the urge to instantly deny her accusation and consider whether it might be true. "Maybe."

She nods. "Then perhaps you should give him some time. He might grow on you."

The idea sits a little uneasily, but mostly because I think she might be right. Nikare is good at everything so far. His father has been High Priest for over a decade, which gives him the advantage of having lived at the temple for most of his life. He knows the place far better than I do.

Maybe if I do as Neffie suggests and give him a bit more time, I'll find myself learning from him.

Then again, maybe I won't and he'll just annoy me further. There's only one way to find out.

Chapter 6

I push through the door into the living area with Matia following behind me like she's been doing at every opportunity since we met on the Day of Choosing. She's remarkably well-behaved for a jackal, even one who has been raised in a temple specifically to *be* a sacred animal. While I'm grateful she isn't difficult to deal with, I have to wonder why.

"Ani," a voice calls from the left.

I turn to find Djou and a couple of the other apprentices waiting by the entrance to the common room.

"We're about to go play senet, but we need a fourth player, want to join?" Djou asks.

My gaze flicks to the other two, wondering how they feel about their friend's offer. Most of my peers are being cordial to me, but aren't going above and beyond that. Djou seems different. Maybe it's because I offered to cover for him on our first day, or perhaps he's just one of life's friendly people, but he always seems like he wants to make an effort.

"Sure, if you don't mind me joining." A small part of me wants to head back to my room and do some extra studying, especially after spending most of my rest day with Neffie, but I know I need to forge some stronger connections with the other apprentices, especially if I'm planning on staying at the temple long term.

"Great. You know how to play, right?" Djou asks.

I raise an eyebrow. It's unusual for anyone not to know how to play the popular board game. "Yes."

"Good, we can..."

Before Djou can finish speaking, one of the temple scribes enters the foyer and scans the space until his gaze lands on me.

"Ankhesenamun?"

"That's me," I respond, though I'm sure he's already realised that considering I'm the only priestess of any rank currently in residence. "But Ani will do," I add automatically.

He nods. "Hori would like to see you."

I glance over at the other apprentices, already regretting that I can't spend time with them. It would be good bonding to get to know them as a team. "Now?"

The scribe nods. "He's in his office."

"Thank you, I'll make my way over. Sorry I can't stay and play," I say to the others.

"Come find us when you're done," Djou responds. "If we're still playing, you can join us then."

I flash him a reassuring smile. "Thanks, I will." I wave awkwardly at them.

The three trainees disappear into the common room, leaving me and Matia to make our way over to the mortuary offices. It's only when I'm halfway there that I realise she's not supposed to come inside the building. Hopefully, it'll be all right if she's nowhere near the dead bodies. With how well-behaved she is, I find it unlikely that she'll go after one of them anyway, but it's better to be safe.

The offices are surprisingly empty given the time of day. Maybe there's something else going on in the temple that I don't know about.

I arrive at Hori's office quickly enough and knock on the open door.

"Come in," he calls.

I step inside.

"Ah, Ani. Please take a seat." He waves me towards the chair opposite him.

I sit, trying not to let my nerves get the better of me. Is he going to kick me out? I don't think I'm doing that badly. I've managed to keep all my food down while cleaning up some truly disgusting messes, and I've listened when my instructors have been telling me about the various processes we use when embalming. The only thing I'm not as good as some of the others at is lifting stuff, but that's mostly due to them having much stronger muscles than I do.

Matia sits next to me, on alert, but not seeming distressed.

"Don't worry, it's nothing bad," he assures me. "We won't be doing assessments for another month or so."

"Mmhmm," I squeak. Does that mean he thinks I'll be in trouble then?

I push the thought aside. Hori has made it clear that he can be a hard taskmaster, but also fair. It seems like he wants us to succeed. Which makes sense. Our success as students reflects his ability as a teacher.

"I wanted to talk to you about your Blessed studies."

"My what?" I blurt, my surprise getting the better of me.

"Ah, I was warned about this," Hori responds. "We make you all go through the Day of Choosing but don't teach any of you what it means to be Blessed until you have been."

"I thought it was just how the gods made their decisions known," I admit.

"It is. But haven't you ever wondered why the gods choose who they do? Why Anubis chose you?"

"Yes."

"Did you come to a conclusion?"

I shake my head. "A small part of me always thought he was just able to sense how much it would mean to me if I was able to serve him. I've always felt a connection to this temple." Am I saying too much?

I reach down and scratch Matia's head absent-mindedly. It's comforting to be able to touch her this way.

"You have good grades in subjects we normally look for in an apprentice here," Hori says. "If you'd gotten the right selection committee, you might have stood a chance at being sent here anyway."

"Even though I'm a girl?"

He smiles sadly. "That's the reason you'd have had to have the right committee. Many of the people making these decisions are still mired in the old ways and aren't open to change. Thankfully, in a few years, that's likely to shift as more open-minded people start selecting students. Hopefully, after that, we'll see more apprentices chosen based on their aptitudes rather than their gender."

"Why are you telling me this?"

"Because by doing well here, you could be part of what makes the change. I think that's one of the reasons Anubis chose you."

"Only one of them?"

Hori nods. "Blessed have innate magical gifts."

I blink rapidly, trying to process what he's saying.

Magic? Me?

"Are you sure?" I ask. "It's just that I've never done anything anyone would consider magic." Maybe I shouldn't be admitting this, but it's better to be honest.

"That's probably because you're thinking in terms of grand miracles and impressive feats. Blessed magic is more subtle than that, and you won't be able to use it until you've been taught how."

"Oh." I slump back in my chair, trying not to be too disappointed.

"As we don't have a Blessed Mentor here, we've had to send for one from another temple. Your training will start with them once they arrive, but I've been informed that the available tutor is on another assignment, so it'll be a few months until you can start."

"Oh. Okay." Questions race through my mind but I'm not sure if I can ask any of them.

"Until then, you'll continue with your main instruction in the mortuary. I've had good reports from several of the other instructors, and I've been impressed by what I've seen from you so far too. If you keep this up, I can see there being a very promising career for you here at the temple."

His kind words take me off guard and I need a moment to compose myself.

"Thank you. It's an honour to be here."

A genuine smile spreads over Hori's face. "It is," he agrees. "And I'm glad you think so. That's everything, I'll let you know when the other Blessed will arrive. You should go enjoy the rest of your day off."

"I will." I get to my feet and turn towards the door. "Come, Matia."

The jackal springs to her feet, ready to follow me as normal.

Hopefully, when the other Blessed priest arrives, he'll be able to tell me more about the bond I share with the jackal too. She deserves me learning everything I can about her.

I hurry back to the living quarters, debating whether I want to head straight to my room so I can message Neffie about what's just happened, or go to the common room to see if the other apprentices are still playing senet.

As much as I want to spend time talking to my best friend, I know it's important that I forge a closer bond with the other apprentices, especially if I want to continue doing well.

With that in mind, I head towards the common room, fully intending to message Neffie as soon as we all go our separate ways for the night.

Chapter 7

We trudge into the mortuary, none of us looking forward to another day of cleaning up bodily fluids and deposits. I may want to serve Anubis, and I'm happy to do it in any way I can, but this is *not* what I had in mind, I much prefer it when we're scheduled to work with the embalming of animals.

"Morning," Hori says brightly. "You'll be pleased to know you're going to be working with volunteer bodies today."

I try not to let my surprise show on my face. I didn't think we'd be doing that so soon, especially as we were scheduled for clean-up duty today.

"We've paired you off based on the skills your schools reported to us. Djou and Ahmes, you're together. Hannu and Ibi, Ani and Nikare..."

I groan. Why can't I be paired with anyone but Nikare? He loves to use any opportunity to show off, and I've no doubt this is going to be one of them.

And now I have to partner with him.

I glare at the tanned dark-haired apprentice. His family tree is yet another thing he likes to remind us of.

"All right, your bodies are waiting for you in the other room. I want you to remember that each and every one of them has a *ka, ba,* and *akh* that we're expected to honour. They are to be treated with respect. If any of you are seen to be treating them with something other than that, you will be removed immediately and returned to clean-up duty."

I briefly wonder who will be doing that while the ten of us are working with the bodies, but it's best not to dwell on that. It's probably used as a punishment for people at all levels of training.

Hori leads us into the small room off to the side, where five bodies lie, not covered by anything. The familiar chill in the air is almost comforting at this point, even if I know its main purpose is to stave off decomposition.

Nikare and I find our way to the far body, a woman with very pale skin and a bloodied nose.

Maybe *volunteer bodies* is just a fancy way of saying *criminals*. But I doubt it. The official line is that a certain level of criminal forfeits the right to life after death and it's an insult to the gods to send them to the Weighing of the Heart knowing they'll fail.

It's more likely, these bodies belonged to those who were too poor to be able to afford even a partial mummification, but who didn't like the idea of going without completely.

"Stand back, I've got this," Nikare instructs me.

I cross my arms and glare at him. "You're not the only one who's capable, you know."

Shock flits across his face. "I've been watching people do this since I was a child."

"And I've done my research and paid attention to what the priests have been doing while we've been here," I counter. "I'm just as capable. Besides, Hori said that we were paired up based on our records. That means we're either equally as good as one another or equally bad. It's your choice which you want to assume I am, but remember it means you're on the same level."

He snaps his jaw shut. "Fine. We can do it together. What do we do first?"

"I thought you'd been watching these things since you were a child?" I throw at him.

"I have. But I want to make sure *you know.*"

I sigh. The only way he's going to believe I'm capable is if I show him. I suppose at least he's trying to act as if I have a chance of getting things right.

"First, we have to check the chart and see what we're dealing with," I say, trying to trust my instincts but questioning them a little now he has. "There's little point in starting to prepare her until we know what we're dealing with."

His nod is so small that I almost miss it. He *really* doesn't want to admit that I'm right.

I ignore him and make my way to the end of the bench, pulling up the woman's chart and scanning the information there. Her name is blanked out, which is surprising when it's normally such an important part of preparing the dead. But I suppose we technically didn't need it when we were the ones preparing the body itself and not the coffin or Book of the Dead. Those things will fall to one of the junior priests who has chosen a specialism that no longer involves direct contact with the dead. I'm not sure if it's a path that interests me as much as working with the deceased does, but maybe that will change once I've met the Blessed priest and learned more about the magic I'm supposed to have.

"She's being prepped for modern mummification," I say.

Nikare wrinkles his nose. "I don't know why anyone chooses that."

"It's cheaper," I point out. "Not all of us have the choice of going the traditional route." Especially as it's grown more and more costly over the years. Traditional mummification is especially tough in countries like ours where it's always damp, which means it has to be carried out by specialist priests. And almost never by apprentices who have yet to actually deal with a full body. I suppose at least that part is going to change for us now.

"I still don't see the point."

I roll my eyes. "Then you're being an idiot." The words are out before I can stop them.

"If you say so, Ankhesenamun."

"Just call me Ani like everyone else," I mutter.

"Fine. But then you have to call me Nik."

"I can live with that. But it doesn't matter what

your personal feelings on modern mummification are. That's what this person wanted, so that's what we're going to prepare her for," I say sternly. Whatever he thinks, he has to respect the wishes of the deceased. Maybe that's something he still needs to learn.

Modern mummification actually makes our job easier. The modern method doesn't involve removing the organs from the body, which is one less thing for us to worry about. I'm not opposed to cutting someone open, but I don't want to make a mistake and would feel better if there was someone supervising me during that process.

I set the chart down and turn to the stack of equipment on the wheeled table next to us. "I guess we start with the basics and clean her up, then we'll know exactly what we're working with," I say.

To my surprise, Nik nods in agreement. "I'll get us some fresh water if you prepare the sponges."

"Fine by me." I try to keep the surprise out of my voice, but I don't manage. Is he going to be easy to work with after all?

Somehow, I don't think so. This has to be a blip.

I pull out several different-sized sponges and lay them out. I've not had to clean a body before, but I can imagine that having a variety will turn out to be helpful.

Nik returns with a bucket and sets it down on the tray. The two of us work in silence to clean the woman in front of us. The water is slightly warmer than I expect it to be, a thoughtful idea on Nik's part.

He focuses on the woman's arms, leaving me to deal with the face. The blood flakes off, turning the water red as it trickles down onto the mortuary table and towards the drain. There's something soothing about cleaning the nameless woman.

It doesn't take long for the two of us to have cleaned her entire body. I step back, admiring how well the two of us have done. I glance over at the other apprentices, realising I haven't paid them any attention while I've been focusing on the woman. All four of the other pairs seem to have reached the same stage we are, and are looking around nervously, probably because they're dreading the next part of the process.

As if on cue, five junior priests enter the room, wheeling small trolleys with glass containers sloshing with embalming liquid on top of them. The process is so different from everything I've heard about the more traditional mummification process, which is probably down to a whole number of factors, the speed, manpower, and materials being some of them.

I clear my throat uncomfortably. "I guess we need to make the incision now."

"Yes," Nik agrees, not seeming like his normal confident self.

"Do you want to do it?" I ask.

For a moment, I don't think he's going to answer, but then he nods ever so slightly. One of the junior priests with the trollies arrives by our station.

"I'm Bebi," he says, but simply stands back and watches as the two of us ready ourselves for the first part of the process.

"Is there a scalpel?" Nik asks.

I pick one up and hand it to him.

He takes it from me and turns his attention to the body, studying it intently. His hand shakes as he hovers the scalpel over the spot he needs to cut, but he doesn't seem to be able to make it.

"Would you show me how to make the cut?" I ask softly.

Nik's eyebrows shoot up. He probably didn't expect me to ask him to show me anything, but I think he needs a chance to prove he knows it.

"Okay." He gestures for me to join him. "Have you studied the diagrams?"

"Yes. But I've never seen it done."

"I have a few times." It isn't lost on me that a lot of his bravado is gone now it's less theoretical and more about actually looking after a dead body.

"I think we have to cut here, right?" I ask, reaching out to touch the spot where I'm reasonably sure we have to make the incision.

I resist the urge to look over at Bebi for confirmation. They'll have been through this dozens of times, they have to know whether or not we're doing this right. But that's not the point of the exercise.

A shout comes from a few bodies over, drawing our attention away from our bench and to where Hannu and Ibi are struggling with their body. I'm not sure what's gone wrong, but it's making me even more nervous about the incision we have to make.

"That's the right spot," Nik says, turning back to our woman. "And we just have to press down..."

The scalpel slides easily into the flesh. I half expect there to be a large spurt of blood, but that doesn't come. Which makes sense. Without the heart to push it around the body, there's nothing to make it project outwards.

"Step back, please," Bebi instructs. He has a pair of tubes in his hand and makes quick work of attaching them to the body.

I watch carefully, realising this was the first chance we get to learn about how the embalming process itself works.

"Now we need to switch on the machine," he says. "That'll push the embalming fluid through the arteries and the blood out of the veins."

I nod and step back, watching as the process goes ahead. I'm a little at a loss over what to do.

"You need to massage the arms and legs," Bebi says. "And the rest of the body if it needs it."

"Okay." I step closer to the body and pick up one of the arms, carefully doing as instructed. It takes Nik a little longer to join me, but the three of us are soon working in silence.

Diluted blood rolls down the metal of the gurney the body is sitting on, sliding down the drain. It's a surprisingly low-key solution, but it seems to work.

The machine makes a gurgling noise and Bebi with us turns it off.

"What's next?" I ask, looking around for some indication. The others seem to be reaching the same point we are, which isn't much help.

"We need to deal with the internal organs," the priest says, picking up a large metal stick with a pointy end. It doesn't look like something I'd want sticking in me. "This is a trocar. You need to stick it into the abdominal cavity and use it to both remove excess gas and waste, as well as inserting more embalming fluid into it. Which one of you wants to try?" He looks between the two of us.

"I'll do it," I offer despite the nerves welling up inside me. I'm not sure if I can actually do it, but I've got to try.

He hands me the trocar. "Just be careful, I'll get the fluid ready while you do that."

"Won't we need to know how to do that too?" Nik asks.

"You will, but that comes later in your training. For now, just focus on the body," Bebi answers.

I push my doubts to the side and stare down at the stomach of the woman in front of me. My gaze catches on something weird. I lean in and examine it, not too sure what I'm looking at. Neat stitches sew together a small incision just below her belly button. I consider asking Nik to take a look but dismiss it as nothing more than an overactive imagination.

"So I just need to push it in?" I ask.

"Yes. Start with the stomach and go from there," Bebi responds.

I take a deep breath and recall my anatomy lessons, carefully locating where I think the stomach will be and sliding the trocar in.

My heart pounds as it slips through the skin. After it starts to work, I relax a little, repeating the same procedure on the other organs and chest cavity, removing any built-up gas there.

"All right, now remove the trocar and hand it to me and I'll inject the embalming fluid," the priest says.

I do as requested and step back so I can watch the rest of the process. Once this is done, it'll be a simple matter of wrapping the body and readying it for burial. Both of those steps feel easier, though we'll have to wait for one of the special priests to arrive to oversee the process. Even in modern mummification, it's important that the rites are overseen the right way, and this is the way to do it.

"We did a good job," Nik says.

I glance at him out of the corner of my eye, surprised to notice the genuine expression on his face.

"We did. Next time, we'll do an even better one."

He chuckles. "I'm sure we will."

Hmm. Maybe Neffie is right and my frustration about Nikare is purely based on the fact he's got an advantage over me when it comes to being a trainee priest. I don't feel nearly so bad now we've successfully worked together. Time will tell if that's a permanent thing or not.

It could go either way.

Chapter 8

The sacred lake sparkles in the afternoon sunshine. I want to make the most of it by spending some time outside with Matia before I have to head inside for dinner.

As if summoned by my thoughts, Matia bounces up to me with a large stick in her mouth, dropping it by my feet.

"You want to play?" I ask, surprised but willing to give it a go.

She nudges the stick with her nose in what I assume is assent.

"All right." I pick up the stick, getting used to its weight. I bring my arm back and throw it as far as I can.

It takes her a moment to respond, but once she

does, she hurtles after it, going faster than I'd ever imagined possible.

The stick thuds to the ground and she pounces on it before turning and running back to me.

I don't ask if it's what she wants this time and just pick up the stick to throw again. She bounces excitedly, letting me know I've done the right thing.

I throw the stick again, watching as she repeats the case. A wide smile spreads over my face. There's something freeing about standing here and playing with her. Maybe it's how happy she looks as she chases the stick, or it could just be as simple as having some time off to think about and do nothing. Life at the temple isn't any harder than I thought it would be, but that doesn't mean I don't need a rest every now and again.

I lose track of time as we play the game, especially as she doesn't seem to be tiring in the slightest. Some of the other priests and apprentices pass as they go about their days. Some of them are having leisure time like I am, but others are still working. There always needs to be enough people to actually tend to the dead.

A chill wind rips through the air, sending a shiver down my spine. Maybe if I go and get a jumper from my room, I can come back out and play with Matia some more. Though from the way she's running now, it's becoming clear that the jackal is starting to get tired.

"Come on, girl," I call to her.

Just like normal, she trots beside me, eager to go where I do. I hope the Blessed priest Hori mentioned arrives soon because I have a lot of questions about how all of this works and exactly what my bond with Matia is. It's a strange situation I've found myself in, even if it's everything I ever wanted.

We head back to the living quarters at a hurried pace. I'm colder than I thought I was and I want nothing better than to get into bed and curl up under the covers with Matia. It sounds like the perfect way to spend the time before dinner.

I push through the door and into the foyer only to find a small crowd gathered and everyone chatting away.

I scan the faces for someone familiar so I can ask what's going on. Djou catches my eye and waves me over to where he's standing with Hannu and Ibi. I push through the crowd until I'm finally standing with them.

"What's going on? Has something bad happened?" I ask.

"It's the vizier," Ibi answers. "He's dead."

My eyes widen. "Dead? I only found out he might be sick a few weeks ago."

"I didn't even know he was sick at all," Hannu says.

"My friend in Bastet's temple told me," I say by way of explanation.

At least all of this explains why there's a crowd.

"What does it mean for us?" I ask.

Djou shrugs. "No idea. I doubt they'll let us anywhere near the mummification process, but maybe we'll be able to help with some things?"

"Hopefully, it'll be good for our training," Hannu adds.

"You can't say that," Ibi snaps. "The vizier of the entire country is dead. There's going to be a period of mourning and we shouldn't be just focusing on ourselves through the whole thing."

I share a confused look with Djou. Up until now, Hannu and Ibi have seemed like the best of friends, to see them disagreeing is a little jarring.

"Can I have everyone's attention please?" Hori calls out. I didn't even realise he was in the room until now.

Unsurprisingly, the room falls silent. Everyone knows who Hori is and he seems to command a decent amount of respect even amongst the more senior priests. It makes sense to me. He's a firm but fair kind of supervisor that makes it easy for people to listen to him.

"As you may have heard, Kamose, the vizier of the British Isles has died today. As I'm sure you can all imagine, this is going to involve some intense preparations here at the temple. I suggest you all have an early night so you can be ready for what happens in the next week or so," Hori announces. "No one's time off will be affected. If you have rest days coming up, they will still be honoured."

A murmur goes through the room, probably people deciding they're pleased that's going to be the case.

"What does it mean for us though?" I ask my companions. "We don't have the same training as the others."

"I guess we'll find out in the morning," Hannu says. "I think I'm going to do what Hori suggests and go to bed. It's nerve-wracking enough working with the volunteer bodies, I don't want to make a mistake if we're given something more important to do."

"Me too," Djou adds. "Though tomorrow might just be another day of entrail sweeping."

I wrinkle my nose. "I hope not. That's easily my least favourite job."

"I think it's supposed to be," he points out. "I'm sure they're using it to work out which of us doesn't have a stomach for the work. I've already heard Menna talking about withdrawing."

"After only a few months?" I can't keep the shock out of my voice.

Djou shrugs. "I don't think he really wanted to serve the temple. From what he's said, he came here because it was what he was expected to do."

Ah. One of those situations. It's probably better if he leaves rather than taking up valuable resources and time.

"I guess that means there'll be more work for the rest of us," Ibi mutters.

"Not if we manage to stay out of trouble," Djou points out. "The year below us will be going through their Day of Choosing before we know it."

He's not wrong there. It's already been a couple of months since we were assigned to the temple of Anubis, I'm sure the rest of the year will fly by. Not that it means anything. We may be ordained priests at the end of the year, but we'll still have a lot of training to go through, and I suspect that will include plenty of the less desirable jobs in the temple will fall on us.

"I'm heading to my room. I'll see you all at breakfast," Hannu says, waving and making his way through the dispersing crowd.

The rest of us say our goodbyes and head our separate ways.

"Come on, Matia. Let's go get some rest," I say to the jackal waiting patiently by my side. I want to be as ready as possible for whatever tomorrow brings.

Chapter 9

I head towards the mortuary along with the other apprentices. Everyone is tenser than normal on account of the vizier's death and not knowing for sure what that's going to mean, either for us, or our education.

Even Nik's quiet and that says everything. I'm half surprised he isn't talking to us all about exactly what a state funeral is going to entail. Maybe he'll get there once the shock has worn off.

Hori is waiting for us just inside the mortuary doors with a solemn expression on his face. As far as I'm aware, his main job is supervising the people currently training in the temple. Not an enviable position to be in given the circumstances.

"Good morning," he says as we all fall into line

in front of him. "As I'm sure you'll probably have guessed, we're going to be a little busier while some of our top embalmers are focusing on preparing the vizier for his funeral. We were all impressed by how you've been handling the volunteer bodies, so we're wanting you to take on a bit more responsibility. You'll have junior priests around to be able to check the work you're doing. Some of you will also be approved to work on partial mummifications as well."

My eyes widen. That seems like a big step, especially as it involves cutting the body open, something none of us have done before. I wish they allowed dissection in our anatomy classes, but there aren't enough high-level criminal bodies to do that, and those that exist are given to the trainee doctors to practise on. Something I'll probably be grateful for if I ever need an operation.

But I think we'll be okay. I've seen plenty of it done here, and I suspect the junior priests will walk us through it.

"All right, to your stations, you'll be collected when someone needs you, but I expect all of you to be busy even when you're not explicitly needed. This is a chance for the ten of you to prove to the temple that you have what it takes." Hori dismisses us and we make our way over to the cleaning stations.

I hope I don't have to be here long. If we're allowed to have more responsibility, then it wouldn't be fun to get stuck cleaning up mortuary tables and dealing with rotting guts.

But I'm not going to complain out loud, especially not when there are people listening in.

I lose myself in the routines of the work, making sure I make everything as spotless as possible. No one says anything, I think we're all hoping that we'll attract the attention of one of the priests doing something interesting.

"Nikare, Ani, can you come join me please?" someone says.

I look up to find the junior priest who worked with us the other day standing close by. What was his name?

Oh, right, Bebi.

I make my way over to him, trying to decide whether I'm more nervous or excited to have been called.

"You're going to come and assist me on a partial mummification," he says. "Pay close attention and do everything I tell you to." The threat that something bad would happen if we don't do what he says lingers under his words.

Though I suspect bad is just that we'd be on clean-up duty for longer. I don't intend to let that happen. Luckily, I doubt Nik will either.

We follow Bebi over to a mortuary table with an elderly man lying prone on it and a trolley next to it filled with the various tools we'll be needing.

"What do you know about partial mummification?" Bebi asks.

"It's the cheapest option," I supply. "Other than that, I'm not sure."

Bebi nods. "As expected. A lot of families don't consider it as an option until they hear about the costs involved in embalming. Even after that, some people opt to donate their bodies for training rather than go through partial mummification."

I glance at Nik from the corner of my eye, half expecting him to say something about how much disdain he feels for the process, but he wisely keeps silent. I have no idea if he's actually re-evaluated some of his thoughts, if he never really thought them in the first place, or if he's just figured out that sometimes it's better to keep quiet. I don't suppose it matters so long as he doesn't insult people.

"The first thing we need to do is take a cast of

the man's face," Bebi says. "You'll find the materials in the first bucket. You should lay a piece of linen over his head first."

I make the assumption that his words are also instructions and make my way over to the equipment he's indicated. I take a piece of dry linen and lay it over the man's face. A bucket of plaster-soaked linen strips sits next to it. I look around for gloves, but don't find any. I'll just have to make sure to wash my hands properly after.

I dip my hand in and pull out one of the strips. It's a little slimy to touch, but I know it'll dry harder. Slowly, I lay it on top of the man's face and smooth it down. I've done this countless times while at school, though never one an actual dead person before.

"Why are we doing this?" Nik asks.

For a moment, I think it's disdain coming from him, but judging from the way he's watching me lay the plaster-soaked linen on the man's face, I don't think it is.

"There are two potential reasons," Bebi responds. "If the family wish to bury the body and let it decompose, then it will be used to create a death mask that will stay with him."

"And if they don't choose to bury the body?" I ask.

"Then the mask is used by the craftsmen creating the canopic jar in which the heart will be laid to rest," Bebi responds with a surprising amount of patience.

"What happens to the bodies that people don't want to bury?" This time, it's clear Nik's question is coming from a place of curiosity. I'll admit to being impressed that he seems to have lost some of his arrogance already. Perhaps it's the sheer amount of hard work we've all had to put in that's rid him of some of his previous notions.

"Various things," Bebi responds.

I frown. Something about the way he says it doesn't sound right. Maybe it's because it isn't a straightforward answer, or maybe I'm seeing problems where there shouldn't be any. I focus on smoothing over a new strip of linen so Bebi can't see my face.

"Some are donated to the medical schools, others are cremated. A rare few are fed to the sacred animals in select circumstances, but the deceased has to have arranged all of that before they die," he continues.

Ah, clearly I'm just seeing things when there's nothing to see. I shouldn't jump to conclusions.

Bebi moves to the end of the bench and picks up the chart with all of the man's notes.

"Nik, we need a heart scarab amulet from the store. The most basic one. Can you collect that along with a plain canopic jar with a temporary lid?"

Nik does a double-take, as if not expecting to be asked to do something like that. "Of course." He disappears to complete his errand.

I continue layering the man's face with the linen strips, making sure to get it as even as possible.

"You're doing a good job," Bebi assures me. "This is something you'll have to do no matter the level of mummification. With the modern method, you can do it afterwards, but with the traditional, natural, and partial methods you need to do them at this stage or you'll end up with something that doesn't resemble the original person. Trust me, you don't want to make that mistake."

"Did you?" The question is out before I can think better of it.

To my surprise, Bebi chuckles. "No, but one of the apprentices who started with me did. He isn't a priest now."

"Just for that mistake?" That doesn't bode well for any of us.

"Oh no, he wasn't cut out for any of it. That was just an example of the kind of mistake he made. We all used to dread being paired with him. The temple I trained at didn't have the same system of pairing up apprentices based on aptitude."

We lapse into silence as I finish the cast of the man's face.

"What do I do now?" I ask, checking over it for any indication that I've missed a spot.

"Leave it to dry. We'll do the rest of what we need to while it sets."

I make my way over to the sink at the end of the bench and wash my hands, scrubbing them hard enough that the stray bits of plaster wash away.

Nik reappears and sets down a simple jar which is slightly slimmer at the top than at the bottom, with a plain lid. From what Bebi told us, I'm guessing a carving of the man's face will end up on top.

He sets a plain scarab down next to it, though I'm sure if I turn it over I'll find hieroglyphics on the bottom. It's the most basic one we offer and is mass-produced in the thousands. Some people don't like the idea that each one isn't hand-carved and carefully created for the deceased, but for others, this is their only chance at being buried with one.

"Right, now we start with the partial embalming," Bebi says. "Though it would be more accurate to call it heart embalming as that's the only thing we do anything with. We're going to use the same solution that we would in the modern method, but in a more concentrated mixture. Sometimes, the heart is also set in resin to protect it more."

He taps a shallow tub of embalming fluid. It's just deep enough to submerge a heart in, but no more than that.

"Watch how I do it," Bebi instructs as he picks up a scalpel and places it against the bottom of the man's neck. Slowly, he draws it down the chest and across the stomach.

My eyes are wide as he pulls the skin back, revealing the bone and flesh beneath. He saws through the bone, carefully moving the various organs to the side until he's at the point where he can sever the tissue holding the heart in place.

He lifts it out and places it in an empty tray. He picks up a smaller version of the trocar he taught us how to use before and carefully slides it into the heart. Congealed blood leaves it and plops onto the shiny surface of the tray below.

"Once we've removed all of the leftover blood, we need to wash the heart," he says, gesturing to the sink. "Nik, if you want to do the honours?"

"Of course." He rushes forward and takes the heart, rinsing it under the water.

He's surprisingly gentle with it, making sure not to do any damage. I watch the way his hands move, impressed by the reverence he's showing.

"That's great," Bebi says, indicating that he's cleaned it enough.

Nik turns off the water and pats the heart dry. Now that it's out of the body, it's hard to think of it as connected to the man lying on the table. I know that's not how I'm supposed to feel, but maybe it's part of my coping mechanism for dealing with the part of my calling that involves cutting up dead bodies.

Bebi takes the heart over to the dish with the embalming fluid in it. Gently, he lowers the heart and leaves it to soak.

"Now we move on to the next body while we wait for the plaster to finish setting and the heart to soak up some of the embalming fluid," Bebi instructs. "Any instruments you've used should be put into the nearest sharps bin. They'll be taken for sterilisation at the end of the day. Never use the same scalpel or trocar on two different bodies. Always wash your hands thoroughly between them."

We nod along but don't say anything. A part of me feels like I'm being thrown into things without enough instruction, and judging from Nik's silence, he probably feels the same.

"Once the process has finished, we'll seal the heart in the canopic jar and pack it up with the plaster cast of the man's face to send to the burial preparation priests who will deal with the rest," Bebi says. "But until then, we shouldn't waste time and need to move on to the next one."

Without further ado, Bebi leads us on to the next body and the process begins again. I don't know if it's a coincidence that so many people today are having partial mummifications, or if it's planned this way, but by the end of the day, I may have a grasp on it.

At least Bebi seems to have the patience to teach us, and Nik is choosing to let his arrogant side have a rest. I hope that continues, I actually don't mind being around him when he's not being obnoxious.

Chapter 10

I glance towards the storeroom door to make sure no one is watching and duck behind one of the large storage tubs just in time to hide the yawn overtaking me. Calling the past few weeks hectic is a bit of an understatement. With many of the more senior priests still tied up in the seventy-day traditional mummification process for the vizier, and an unexplained slightly higher than normal death rate, we've been kept on our toes helping the junior priests keep up with the modern and partial mummifications. I've even performed a couple of the latter on my own now, which was terrifying.

But it's left me exhausted, and I'm almost glad to have been assigned the job of collecting amulets for the morning. It doesn't take as much brain power, and if I get it wrong, it's easy to fix, unlike cutting open a body.

Satisfied my yawn has passed, I go back to collecting the various amulets and statuettes along with the roll of linen Hannu and the junior priest he's assisting need. We're still not allowed to wrap the bodies, but we get to watch it being done now.

Confident that I've collected everything I need, I head back out into the main room, only to almost run straight into Nik.

I lose my balance only for him to reach out and steady me.

"Thanks," I murmur.

"No problem. Are you okay?" Something akin to genuine concern flits over his face. He's definitely come a long way since the start of our training. Maybe he always needed a chance to get it out of his system. Or perhaps it's simpler than that and he just needed to discover for sure that he wasn't going to be treated any differently just because of who he is.

I nod. "Just a bit tired. Tomorrow can't come soon enough."

"Ah, you have a rest day?"

I nod.

"Me too, maybe we should..."

Before he can finish his suggestion, the doors sweep open and several people walk in. Beside me, Nik tenses.

My gaze lands on High Priest Ahmose and the pieces fall into place. He may have been nice to me after the Day of Choosing, but I bet he's been hard on Nik his entire life.

A small part of me wants to reach out and place a comforting hand on Nik's arm, but I refrain. We don't have that kind of friendship.

"Ah, Nikare, you're here," the High Priest says. "Excellent timing. I'm sure you remember our esteemed guest, His Highness Prince Ramesses."

My eyes widen. I can't say I ever expected to meet the prince of the entire empire while standing in a room with over a dozen dead bodies.

"Your Highness," Nik says, dipping his head.

"And this is our Blessed Apprentice, Ankhsenamun," Ahmose adds.

Oh no, he's introducing me too? Couldn't it have waited until I was wearing a nice dress with my hair and makeup done rather than wearing clothes covered in the grime of the day and my hair thrown back into a haphazard ponytail? I don't normally care about these things too much, but meeting a member of the royal family is definitely a special occasion.

Mum would be mortified if she found out what state I'm in right now.

"It's a pleasure to meet you," Ramesses says. "Why don't the two of you give me a tour of the mortuary so we can let the High Priest get back to his duties?"

From the expression on the High Priest's face, I can tell he isn't particularly happy about that turn of events, though I suspect it's not because he doesn't trust us and just because he'd hoped to spend some time making a good impression on the prince himself.

But a suggestion from a royal isn't something he can ignore. Even I know that.

"Yes, the two of them can take it from here," Nik's father responds. "You can send for me when you're done and I can escort you to the feast."

"That would be excellent, thank you." Ramesses gestures to his guards, dismissing them quickly.

"I need to go deliver this to Hannu," I whisper to Nik, gesturing to the basket.

He nods. "I'll entertain His Highness until you get back." There's something about the way he says the words that makes it clear he's not happy.

"I won't be long," I promise, already making a move.

I hurry through the mortuary to the table I'm supposed to deliver to.

"I'm so sorry, I was given an assignment by the High Priest," I say to the junior priest Hannu is assisting.

The man just grunts.

"Sorry," Hannu mouths at me.

"It's okay," I respond equally silently. He's told me about this junior priest before, and he hates working with him.

"What have you been asked to do?"

"Give Prince Ramesses a tour of the mortuary," I respond to Hannu.

"The prince is here?" He doesn't bother hiding his surprise.

"Apparently. I'll try and find out as much as I can and report back over dinner."

He chuckles. "You'd better. Good luck."

"Thanks. I really should get back, I've left the prince alone with Nik."

"Definitely hurry. Don't let him mess anything up for you "

I want to tell him that Nik would never do that,

but I don't have any evidence to back that up other than my gut.

I wave to my fellow apprentice and hasten my way back to the two men waiting for me.

If anything, Nik seems to have become even tenser since I left, especially if the set of his mouth is anything to go by.

"I'm sorry about that, Your Highness, I had to finish the errand I was running," I say a little breathlessly.

"It isn't a problem, Ankhsenamun. But please, call me Ramesses." He reaches out and takes my hand in his, lifting it to his mouth and placing a gentle kiss there.

I resist the urge to blush. "Only if you call me Ani," I mumble.

"Is that what your friends call you?"

"More like everyone," I respond truthfully.

"Then lead the way, Ani."

Something about the way he smiles makes him a lot less intimidating. Perhaps if I can remember to call him Ramesses, I'll stop seeing him as so far above me and relax.

"What is it you'd like to see?" I ask.

"Everything. This is the first time I've visited your temple," he responds.

"What made you choose now to change that?"

"My father asked me to represent him at the vizier's funeral. I arrived yesterday and wanted to get the lay of the land before I throw myself into preparations," Ramesses says.

"So you're going to be here for a while?" Nik asks stiffly. I haven't heard him sound like this since the first week.

"A couple of months at the least. Father wants me to stay until after the next vizier is elected to help smooth over the transition. I'm more than happy to oblige."

I resist the urge to frown. Something about the way he's saying things makes it sound fake, but I can't put my finger on what it is. Perhaps it's just because he's used to talking to the court and not to people like us.

"Shall we begin the tour?" he asks.

"Of course. Follow us." I try and recall everything Hori told us on the first day so I can relay it to the prince, and hopefully, I don't miss anything. The last thing I want to do is make a bad impression on someone as important as this.

Chapter 11

I rub my arm across my eyes, trying to rid myself of the vague sting there. It's been a long day after a whole host of other long days and if it were up to me, I would be heading straight home to rest. But with the hecticness throughout the temple, I know that isn't possible and it's down to the ten of us to clear down after a day full of embalming.

I pick up a stray trocar, and having no idea whether or not it's been used, drop it into the nearest sharps bin. Ibi will be along in a few minutes to pick it up and take the contents to be sterilised.

"Ani, have you got a minute?" Nik asks softly, still taking me by surprise and making me jump. "Sorry," he adds.

I turn to face him and try to offer him a reassuring smile. "It's okay, I just wasn't expecting you.
What's up?"

"Can you come look at something for me? I
want a second opinion."

"And you want it to be mine?"

He frowns. "Why wouldn't I?"

I can think of at least a dozen reasons, but it
seems like most of them are my insecurities and not
things he's thinking.

"Okay." I set down my cleaning equipment,
admittedly intrigued by what he wants.

He nods and turns to walk in the direction of
the body fridges.

I frown, unsure what he wants me to check on.
I hurry after him, only catching up as he pulls
open the door of one of the fridges and steps
inside.

"If you're going to kill me, this probably isn't the
best place for it," I quip. "There are a lot of
witnesses."

He chuckles deeply. "Oh, I know. If I wanted to
kill someone, I'd wait until the deep of winter and
push them into the Thames."

"Smart. But now I know that's your plan, isn't
that dangerous?"

He winks. "Not if you're near the river in a couple of months."

A soft snort of amusement escapes me. "And now I know to avoid going anywhere near you and water at the same time."

The grin on his face suggests he's enjoying this as much as I am.

"But why have you brought me to the fridge?" I ask, a little bit more seriousness slipping in.

"Have you ever seen something suspicious here?" he asks.

"Suspicious like you leading me into a fridge without telling anyone else where we're going, or something different?"

His lips twitch and amusement dances through his eyes, but it disappears quickly. "Something seriously suspicious."

I raise an eyebrow. "I'm intrigued. Why are you asking?"

"I was moving a body the other day and I found something, but I'm not sure if I'm being paranoid."

"If you're asking for my opinion on it, then I think you've already decided on that," I point out.

"Fair."

The chill air of the huge fridge travels right through me. Normally, only wearing one layer of clothing isn't a problem. Not when I spend most of the day running around. But the fridge is a different matter, and it's already starting to cut through the thin material of my shirt.

"Have you dealt with the organ shelf yet?" he asks.

I shake my head. "I'm guessing it's just what it sounds like."

He nods. "But there's something strange about it."

"All right, show me what's going on."

"Here." He points to a pot labelled kidneys.

I frown and step forward and pull open the lid. The metallic scent of liver assaults me almost instantly.

"That's not right," I mutter.

"No, it isn't. And it's not the only one," Nik says darkly. "I've seen it happen a couple of times. I mentioned it to Bebi, but he just dismissed it and said he'd sort the labels out."

"Did he?"

"I don't know. When I came to check the next day, the container was gone."

"That's strange. Why is there even an organ shelf? Don't most of them stay with the body?" Or end up in the incinerator after we've cleared things up.

"Most, but a handful are removed and sent to the doctors for transplants."

"Oh right, I forgot about that. But mislabelling them isn't going to get the right thing to the right place."

"No, it won't," he agrees. "And if it was once, I'd dismiss it as a mistake."

I put the lid back down, resisting the urge to look in more of the boxes. "How many times has it happened?"

"At least once a week. I haven't had a chance to check more often than that."

"That's a lot of mislabeled organs," I mutter. "Someone must either be really incompetent at their job..."

"Or they're doing it on purpose," he finishes for me. "Have you noticed anything weird on any of the bodies?"

I frown, remembering a few incidents where things haven't quite added up. "Remember the first one we worked on together? I thought she had a weird surgical wound. Maybe we should check some of the others who have been marked for modern mummification?" Though even as I'm saying it, I don't know what any of that proves.

"Want to have a look?" He gestures towards where the bodies are stored.

I glance over my shoulder to check none of the other apprentices are paying us any attention, but they all seem busy with their tasks.

"All right, but we should be quick. If either of us catch hypothermia, it'll raise suspicions."

"True."

We make our way over to the section dedicated to tomorrow's bodies.

"You take this end, I'll take the other and we'll meet in the middle?" Nik suggests.

I nod and turn my attention to the first body. The paperwork says he's going to go through a partial mummification, so I skip him and move on to the next.

After checking five bodies and not finding any signs of tampering, I'm about ready to give up and get out of the fridge.

"I got something," Nik calls.

I recover the body in front of me and hurry over to him.

"Look, here." He points out an incision line just below the belly button.

"Could it just be a medical procedure that caused it?" I ask.

"Not according to the notes."

I frown. "One of us can try and get assigned to the body tomorrow?" I suggest.

"I'm not sure what that will do," he says glumly.

"Probably nothing," I admit. "But at least it means we can ask some questions?"

"I suppose."

I reach out and touch his arm gently. "We can keep investigating," I promise. "We'll keep an eye on anything we think is suspicious. If we're watching, then we're bound to come across something sooner rather than later, and once we do, we can report it to Hori or your father, or someone who will listen."

Relief flashes over Nik's face. "Thank you for believing me."

I do a double-take. "Why wouldn't I?"

"No reason," he mumbles. "But I'm still grateful to have someone who will help me keep an eye on things."

"No problem. Something doesn't feel right about the situation. But we're smart, we'll figure it out."

"You think I'm smart?" He raises an eyebrow.

"Don't be coy, it doesn't suit you. We both know you're intelligent, there's no denying that."

"Fair point."

"We should get out of here before anyone gets suspicious about where we've gone or I catch a chill. I don't particularly want to be stuck in my room for the next week, it sounds a little dull."

He snorts. "That's fair. Next time I want you to meet me secretly in the walk-in fridge I'll make sure to bring a blanket."

"That sounds suspiciously like a secret rendezvous," I mutter.

"What was that?" he asks.

"Nothing. Just my teeth clattering," I say hastily, not wanting to put any ideas in either of our minds.

We both do a scan of the inside of the fridge to make sure nothing is out of place before we leave. If we're going to work out what's going on, then we can't leave any clues that we know something is wrong. That's a good way for whoever is to blame for the situation to learn to cover their tracks better.

And that's not what we want.

Chapter 12

It's hard to believe a whole seventy days have passed since news of the vizier's death spread through the temple. And after a long mummification process, he's ready to be laid to rest in one of the biggest funerals the country has seen in recent history. I'm actually not completely sure what to expect, only that I'm expected to attend along with the rest of the priesthood, and that Matia should come with me.

A knock pulls my attention to my door.

I pull it open to find a man I've never seen on the other side.

"Can I help you?" I ask.

"Are you Ankhsenamun?"

I resist the urge to roll my eyes. I know it's polite

to double-check, but I'm literally the only woman living in this part of the building, it's not that much of a surprise who I am.

"Yes."

"I have a package for you." He holds out a brown box.

I frown. "I'm not expecting anything."

"It's from Priest Inkaef. He looks after the sacred jackals."

"Oh." So it's something to do with Matia, that's reassuring.

"He thought you'd need special garments for the funeral," the man says, handing the box to me.

"Thank you. Please tell him that I appreciate it."

He nods and turns to leave.

I close the door and set the box down on my desk so I can open it. Inside sits a gold collar and what looks like four bracelets, though they're too small for my wrists.

I glance at Matia. She's busy licking her paws and isn't paying any attention to the box or my visitor.

"Some guard jackal," I mutter.

Except that he said he was coming from Priest Inkaef, which means he's probably worked with the sacred jackals, including Matia who lived there up until she moved in with me several months ago. I do wonder if she misses being around the others sometimes, but she seems happy enough.

"I guess I'm not the only one who has to dress up today," I say out loud.

She looks up, having heard me speaking but having no idea what I mean. I make my way over to her and set the box down.

I slide the gold collar around her neck and snap it shut. It fits well and doesn't look restrictive at all. She certainly doesn't seem bothered by it.

"Can I put these around your paws?" I ask, holding up the bracelets. I'm not sure why I'm asking her when she can't really understand, but it feels right to.

Carefully, I clip one around each of her legs and step back. She looks like she's walked straight out of one of the wall paintings.

I get to my feet and turn my attention to myself. She's not the only one who needs to look their best today. I open the wardrobe and searched through the clothing hanging there until I find the stiff white linen formal dress I'm expected to wear today. Months of not having a reason to need to wear it haven't improved my attitude towards it.

I pull it out, scanning it quickly to make sure

there aren't any stains or damage on it. The last thing I want is to turn up wearing something that'll embarrass the temple.

The dress fits well, hugging my body in just the right way. The inner sheath clings to my body in a way that natural linen doesn't. I'm fairly sure they must mix it with something else to get it to behave that way. The outer dress floats around my shoulders in a sheer outer garment. I turn to catch sight of myself in the mirror.

The dark eyeliner and the styled hair take me off guard for a moment. After spending most of the past few months leaning towards practical clothing and my hair tied up, it's almost strange to see myself this way.

The only thing left to do is put on my jewellery.

I unclip the lid of the box holding my collar and bracelets. They were a sixteenth birthday present from my parents and some of my most treasured possessions, even if I don't get to wear them very often.

I slide the bracelets over my wrists and attach the collar into place. It lies heavily against my chest even if parts of it are made of lighter materials. Some of the jewels are fake, and others are only semi-precious stones, but the craftsmanship is good enough that no one will notice and the colours stand out well against the white of my dress.

"All right, I guess that's us done," I say to Matia. "Shall we go?"

As if understanding what I'm saying, she gets to her feet.

I lock my door and slip my key into the small pocket in my dress that was probably designed for this purpose. Like with the Day of Choosing, I can't bring anything else with me, which means my phone and money have to stay behind. Though as I'm not leaving the temple grounds, I don't suppose that matters much.

I make my way down to the foyer where the rest of the apprentices are waiting. We're only watching from the sidelines for this funeral, but in the future, we may get to take part.

Djou waves me over as soon as he sees me and I hurry to join them.

The moment I step into his line of sight, Nik stops talking and just stares at me.

"Did you forget I'm a girl?" I tease.

He chuckles. "Not at all. It's just odd seeing you so dressed up."

"Likewise."

The jewelled collar around his neck is bigger

than mine, and I suspect more of the jewels are real. One of the perks of being the son of someone important. Though I'll admit that it isn't his jewellery choices that have caught my attention, but the bare chest beneath it.

"You look good," he says.

"You do too." Which isn't a word of a lie.

"Have you seen anything else suspicious?" he asks.

I glance around to make sure none of the other apprentices are listening to us, but they're all preoccupied with their own conversations.

"No more than we know already."

Disappointment flits over his face, but it vanishes a moment later. It's not like he didn't know what my answer was going to be. We've both been keeping an eye out, but all we've found so far is exactly the same as what we noticed in the fridge. There have been some more mislabelled organs and strange incisions on bodies, but that's it. I wish we'd found more.

Before we can discuss it further, we're herded out of the door and into our places. I'm more nervous than I want to admit about what's going to happen next. We don't even have to do anything, but it's still the first time I'm representing the temple in public, and with Matia by my side, everyone's going to know who I am.

But it's going to be fine. Especially when I'll be standing with the rest of the apprentices. They've all made me feel welcome among their number, even if they were hesitant at first. I hope that continues into the future too, though I have no reason to think it won't. Even Nik's come around to me being here.

Chapter 13

The beat of drums and the wail of the formal mourners are the first indications that the funeral procession has nearly reached us. Once they enter the temple, they'll head into the peristyle courts where we're all waiting for them so a performance of the story of Osiris and Seth is put on for all of us gathered. Despite the story of the rivalry between the two brothers is well known throughout the empire, it's often included in the funeral rites.

After they're done, the procession will continue through the temple and out of the gate at the other end for the coffin to be loaded onto a boat to be taken to its final resting place where High Priest Ahmose will perform the opening of the mouth ceremony.

I've seen smaller funerals before, but nothing on this scale.

I reach down and scratch Matia's head. I'm glad to have her with me, even with all the people around.

The first mourners enter the open-air peristyle court. The women appear wild with their hair messed up and their clothes torn. They beat against their chests as they wail and scream. I have no idea if they're professional mourners or members of the vizier's family, but I suppose it doesn't matter. Whichever is the case, they are performing the job they're supposed to.

Despite the erraticness of their movements, there's something almost hypnotic about the way they move. From the way they're working together, I have to come down on the side of them being professionals.

The coffin arrives next, drawn by a huge pair of oxen. Once it's in place, the mourners step to the side and priests trained in acting begin to portray the story of Osiris and Seth.

Despite knowing the story well, I'm as enraptured as everyone else as the priestess playing Isis lets out a grieved scream over the death of Osiris.

A hand touches my arm, making me jump.

I turn to find Nik next to me.

"We should go," he whispers.

I raise an eyebrow. "We're in the middle of the funeral," I point out, keeping my voice low so I don't call attention to us.

"Which is going to be the best time to investigate what's going on in the mortuary," he points out. "No one else is going to be there unless they're up to no good. This is our chance to find out what's actually going on."

I chew on my bottom lip. It's a huge risk. If we're caught, someone might think we're up to no good. "Won't we get into trouble?"

"I can talk us out of it if we do," he promises.

My gaze flickers to his father standing next to the coffin as the play continues. His attention isn't on what's going on with his priests. In all likelihood, no one will even notice if we slip away. People are coming and going to get refreshments and use the bathroom, we won't raise any eyebrows.

I sigh. Nik's right. If anyone is up to no good, this is when they're going to make a move. Most of the temple staff are congregated here right now. Anyone staying behind will be fairly easy to bribe or manipulate. Not by us, but by whoever it is mislabelling the organs. And there's no way of knowing when we're going to get another chance to find out what's going on.

"Okay."

"That was easier than I thought."

I raise an eyebrow. "To convince me to come with you? You're making a good point."

"Careful, Ani, that's almost a compliment. I thought you didn't like me."

"I find you tolerable," I tease. "Less so when you're gloating."

A triumphant grin spreads over his face. "We should go before you change your mind."

I nod, trying my best to ignore the nerves fluttering inside me. Maybe it's reckless of me to follow along with his plan, but despite my reservations when I met him, I trust his judgement. He's competent at what he does, and he noticed something bad was going on just from a few errors. No one else has or they would have put a stop to it already.

Nik pushes his way through the crowd. It's easy enough to move through them after him, even with Matia following at my heels. Though maybe she makes it easier when people decide they don't want to have their hands bitten or something. Not that she'd do that, but I understand why people might think that, especially if they haven't come across a sacred jackal before.

I keep an eye on the people around us as we make our way towards the mortuary.

The closer we get, the more nerves make themselves known, and the horrible thought of if no one has stopped this before, maybe it's because the higher-ups know about it already.

My gaze slips to Nik.

Wouldn't he already know if his father was involved? I'm not sure. Sometimes, they seem close to one another, and other times they don't. I haven't been in a position to ask him much about his family. We're not that kind of friends.

Voices sound from the mortuary door.

Nik grabs hold of my arm and pulls me to the side. Matia follows, pushing herself up against my leg as if she knows how important it is to stay by my side.

The pair of priests pass and head towards the ceremony.

"Ready?" Nik asks.

"Is it bad to say I'm not sure?"

He chuckles. "I get it," he promises. "We can go back to the funeral if you prefer."

As much as I appreciate his offer, I know we can't do that. Not when there's something so wrong going on.

"It's fine. Let's just get in there and see what we can find out."

He nods and leads the way inside.

It's eerily quiet in the mortuary. While there are still bodies in the fridge, they're waiting for the next stage of their mummification but the priests who do the work aren't around. I don't think I've ever seen the place this quiet before.

"What do we do now?" I ask Nik.

"I honestly don't know," he admits. "I've never snuck into a mortuary to do some sleuthing before."

"Then I guess we will learn together." I offer him a reassuring smile, getting one in return. "Wait, what's that?" I point to the gurney nearest the fridge which seems to have a small selection of boxes sitting on it. They weren't there when we cleaned down the night before.

"No idea."

We make our way towards it, both of us trying to keep an eye on our surroundings. Somehow, I don't think being caught by someone like Nik's father or Hori is going to be as much of a problem as if we're caught by the people who are up to no good.

Matia trots over with us, stopping to sniff every now and again but not running off to try and eat anything, which I know has been a lot of people's concerns about having her in here. Perhaps I should have asked her to stay outside, but it's too late now.

"Do you want to stand guard or open the boxes?" Nik asks.

"The opening, if you don't mind." A small part of me doesn't trust my observation skills when it comes to keeping an eye on the front door.

"You got it." He steps back and puts himself facing the door. "Want to help, Matia?" he asks the jackal.

She gives a small yip that I assume is consent. Her ears prick up and her whole body stills as if she really is on high alert.

I take a deep breath and open the first box to find a liver inside it. I check the label, unsurprised to find *kidneys* written on it instead.

"Not what it's supposed to be," I mutter.

"I didn't think it would be."

Me neither.

The next box contains a set of lungs, and

another one has another liver in it. Despite the labelling, there aren't any kidneys. I wonder if that's purposeful or if more people are just willing to donate them.

A loud gasp escapes me as I pull the lid off the final box.

"What is it?" Nik asks when I don't tell him.

"A heart." My voice is so faint that it's almost impossible to make out my own words. "They've stolen a heart."

"It could just be donated." There's a hesitancy in his voice that says he doesn't really believe that. It isn't surprising. All of these organs are stolen, the heart isn't going to be any different.

Heart transplants are rare due to a lack of donors, though doctors have been working on alternative treatments in order to make up for the loss. None of that changes that removing the heart from someone without a dozen signed forms is highly illegal.

Illegally obtained hearts probably sell for a small fortune on the black market, and now we're in the way of whoever is responsible for this.

Something tells me that's not a good place to be.

Matia lets out a slight growl and paws in the direction of the door.

"Get the lid back on," Nik whispers.

Hastily, I press it down and make sure everything is in place.

The door to the mortuary opens and my eyes widen. What are we going to do now? We're literally standing over someone's stash of stolen organs. They're either going to try and drag us into the operation, or we'll end up hurt in the process.

I don't particularly want either.

"Ani, get in here," Nik says, waving towards the now-open fridge door.

I glance between the mortuary entrance and where we are now but realise this is our only option if we don't want to get caught.

Voices fill the room just as Nik pulls me inside.

"Matia," I blurt, starting to head back outside.

Nik tugs me back and shuts the door. "She's smart and small. She'll be okay," he promises.

I bite my bottom lip, wishing I could go out and make sure my jackal is okay, but knowing it's dangerous to do that. And Nik is right. Matia is both smart and capable of hiding. I'm sure she's done the same.

But that's not going to stop me worrying about her.

A shiver runs through my body as the chill of

the fridge sets in. Formal clothing isn't a good fit for being in a fridge either.

"Sorry I forgot the blanket," Nik jokes.

The corners of my lips quirk into an amused smile. "Hopefully we won't have to be in here long."

And only partly because we'll get sick.

Chapter 14

My teeth chatter from the cold despite pacing up and down, and the temptation to steal one of the modesty sheets from one of the many dead bodies in the fridge is growing by the moment.

But I resist.

I long to leave and find out if Matia is okay. But I'm also glad she's not in here getting too cold. I have no idea if she'd be able to withstand it. Especially when we can barely manage ourselves.

"How long do you think it's going to be before it's safe?" I ask Nik.

"I have no idea," he admits. "We might have only been in here for a few minutes as far as I can tell."

"Eurgh. I hate that there's no place for a phone in our formal wear."

"I know, it's impractical. One tiny pocket just isn't enough."

"You should try finding regular women's clothing with more than that," I mutter. "It's all like formal wear. One of the many reasons I'm glad to be here and not training to be a priestess somewhere else."

Nik chuckles. "Is that what you spend your time thinking about?"

"Not really," I admit.

"I'm sorry I don't have a blanket this time."

A soft snort escapes me. "I don't expect you to carry one around just in case we get stuck in a fridge while hiding from organ thieves."

"Still. I promised and I didn't deliver."

"Then next time you'll need to bring two blankets to make up for it."

"Deal."

The creak of the fridge handle stops our conversation in its tracks. We exchange a worried glance before searching for a better place to hide.

"Under the gurney," Nik says, pointing to the nearest dead body covered in a sheet. It's not the best hiding place, especially when the sheet doesn't touch the floor. But it should do. Especially when no one's expecting to find the living inside a mortuary fridge.

I hope.

We crouch down and crawl under, surprisingly close. At least I get to take advantage of his body heat while we're hiding here.

"We need another heart," a man says.

I recognise the voice, but I'm not entirely sure who it belongs to. I'm better with faces than with voices.

"It's risky," a second man responds. This time I can put a name to him.

Bebi.

I let out a small gasp, only for Nik to place his hand over my mouth.

I nod by way of thanks and he removes it.

"Barely," the first man scoffs. "Everyone is so preoccupied with the funeral that no one will notice if we help ourselves to a heart. We need it if we want to get paid."

"Fine. But be quick and careful about it. The body at the back should be the best choice. It's a volunteer one, so we can tell one of the apprentices to take care of it. Maybe Menna. He spends so much time trying not to throw up that he won't notice the body's been tampered with."

"I don't care which of them we give it to," the first man mumbles.

"You should. Some of them are too clever to be trusted with that. I've already had some of them questioning our incision marks and what they are. I don't think they believed me when I said they were probably operation scars," Bebi says.

I exchange a glance with Nik. There's no way he isn't talking about us.

"Pfft. What's it matter? A group of apprentices aren't going to be able to stop us. If it comes to it, we can just convince them to join us."

"When one of them is the High Priest's son, I don't think that's wise," Bebi counters.

"Or maybe it is. If we can get him involved, we'll be nearly untouchable. The High Priest wouldn't shut us down if his son is involved."

"It's too much of a risk," Bebi snaps. "Just focus on getting the heart so we can get out of here before anyone gets suspicious."

"Fine, fine. But I'm bringing up the High Priest's son with the boss, I think it's a good idea."

On a whim, I reach out and take Nik's hand in

mine, giving it a squeeze. It can't be nice to hear them talk about him like this. Not as if he's a person on his own merit and a capable apprentice, but that he'd be good because of his connections. Despite the way he started out his training here, I don't think he wants to be known for who he is.

We have that in common.

Alarm crosses his face. "I'm going to sneeze." His panicked whisper sends a chill through me.

"Touch your nose," I respond.

"What?"

"It's supposed to help, just do it." Even if it doesn't stop his sneeze, at least we tried.

Nik does as I suggest.

I cross my fingers, hoping it'll work. Any noise is going to get us noticed in a way that isn't going to end well for us.

He shakes his head and I know it's going to be too late. The sneeze escapes from him, though he manages to suppress it the best he can.

"Who's there?" Bebi calls.

I close my eyes. What are we going to do now? I doubt they're going to be happy about being listened to, especially when they were just talking about Nik.

I wish I could ask him what he thinks, but now

the two priests are on alert, any sound will alert them to where we are.

"It was probably one of the bodies, Bebi," the other man says.

"I told you not to use names."

"Even so, you know what they're like. Sometimes they get filled up with gas and groan. That's what we heard."

"Hmm." Bebi isn't convinced. "Leave the heart. We can't risk it if someone is in here."

"We can't. If we don't turn up with two, we're not going to get paid."

"And if we get caught, we're not going to get paid at all," Bebi points out.

"It's worth the risk." The second priest heads deeper into the fridge.

"Fine. But if you're not done in ten minutes, we'll leave without you and you won't get your cut. And you'd better do a sweep of the fridge after to make sure there's no one here."

A violent shiver runs through me as another wave of cold washes over us. Or terror. If the priest even does a half-decent sweep of the fridge, he's going to find us, and I don't know what will happen then.

To my surprise, Nik reaches out and puts an

arm around me. It helps a little, but with how cold he is too, it's not the best. We need to get out of here.

Ideally while stopping the priest from desecrating someone's body too.

"Think we can take him?" I whisper once I'm sure Bebi has left the fridge. I'm trying not to focus too much on the hurt over the person who has been teaching us being the one trading in illegal organs.

"We can try." Nik doesn't seem so sure.

"We can just hide if you think that's better?"

He sighs. "I don't. They need to be stopped. And if we stay here, we're going to get caught anyway. At least this way we stand a chance, especially if they think I'm valuable."

He has a point.

"Okay, then let's do this." I crawl out from under the gurney but stay low to the ground so the priest doesn't see me.

I wish I was wearing my normal clothes instead of a formal dress, it's not the most practical outfit to be doing this in. Though at least I'm more covered than Nik is.

I spot an abandoned organ tray a few feet away and head towards it. While it may not be much in terms of a weapon, it's much better than not having anything to defend myself with.

Nik follows behind me and we crawl further into the fridge. It's good to be moving again, but even if it doesn't completely get rid of the chill in my bones.

A clatter comes from the direction of the priest. He doesn't seem to be having an easy time of it. Which doesn't surprise me. I wouldn't want to be trying to remove an organ at this temperature either.

"Stop what you're doing," Nik shouts as he gets to his feet.

I follow suit, keeping a tight hand on my organ pan just in case I need it.

The priest startles and drops his scalpel, visibly shaking from either cold or fear, it's hard to tell which.

"Step away from the body and I'll tell my father to be lenient on your punishment," Nik continues.

I raise an eyebrow, wondering if he's actually going to stick to that promise. Probably not, but I don't want to ask him and ruin the moment.

The door to the fridge opens and I spin around, only partly prepared for whoever it is on the other side.

"Are you done yet, Minnefer? We really need to get going," Bebi says. His gaze lands on me and Nik. "Ah."

"If you turn yourselves in, Father will be lenient," Nik says, though from his shaking voice, I don't think he fully believes it.

"You don't know what you're dealing with here," Bebi warns. "The two of you should join us. There's a nice payout. Well worth your time."

"No, thank you," I say firmly. "And I suggest you stop what you're doing now."

To my surprise, Minnefer makes a break for it, sprinting towards the door. Neither of us react in time and he slips past, almost running into Bebi, but he moves out of the way so fast that he slams into the door and knocks himself out.

I suppose that saves us a job. I'm not convinced my organ pan would be much use if I actually had to try and incapacitate someone.

We turn our attention to Bebi. So long as he doesn't manage to get the upper hand on us, we should be okay. Minnefer seems like the kind of person who will crack under the slightest bit of pressure.

Bebi seems to figure this out, as he turns and starts to run through the mortuary. Unfortunately for us, he has the advantage of not having spent the last ten minutes in a fridge going numb from the cold. But this is a good chance for us to get out of there.

He slams the fridge door closed, but that's not too much of an issue now he knows we're here. Like all walk-in fridges, this one has a button for it to open from the inside.

Nik gets there first and pushes the door open and we step back into the main room of the mortuary.

Even the comparative warmth of the air outside the fridge is enough to make my skin tingle, and not in a pleasant way. We're going to have to be careful we don't end up sick after this.

Bebi has got a head start on us, so much so, that I realise there's a chance we're not going to catch him.

"Should we let him go and hope Minnefer talks?" I ask Nik.

Uncertainty flits over his face, probably because he feels the same way I do. It would be good if we can apprehend them both, but there's a chance we won't be able to.

A loud almost playful growl sounds and Matia jumps into action.

Relief floods through me at the sight of my jackal safe and well, I was more worried about her than I want to admit.

She bounds after Bebi, chasing him through the mortuary in a way neither of us are capable of. There's a good chance that she's just trying to play with him, but he probably doesn't know that.

"We should tie Minnefer up so he doesn't get away," Nik says.

I nod in agreement. "Then we should get Hori." I pause, considering whether or not it's a good idea to involve our supervisor. Could he be in on it?

"Good idea. If you want to go get him, I'll deal with Minnefer."

I brush a hand against his arm and shoot him a grateful smile. I'm worried about how clammy he feels, but I know there's nothing we can do about it right now. We have to deal with one problem at a time.

I hurry through the mortuary and out into the temple grounds. Horror washes through me as I notice the procession including the coffin heading towards the quay. It's terrible timing that we've managed to clash with them.

I glance in the opposite direction to find Bebi

almost at the temple exit, with Matia hot on his heels.

She pounces, knocking him to the ground. Hopefully, she'll keep him occupied while I go for help.

The other apprentices spill out of the peristyle court entrance and towards the living quarters. This is my chance.

"Djou!" I shout.

He turns, surprise registering on his face as he sees me.

I hurry over, not wanting to shout about what's happening.

"What's wrong? You and Nik disappeared..."

"It's a long story. Do you know where Hori is?"

"He's inside still talking to one of Osiris' priests," he says. "Why?"

"I need to talk to him urgently." I glance over at where Matia is still standing on top of Bebi, licking his face. Ah, so she is playing with him. I bet he feels a little silly right now. "Can you do me a favour?"

"Sure."

"Can you make sure Bebi doesn't escape? It's really important."

Confusion flashes over Djou's face. "Sure. We'll

do that." He gestures to his friends and the three of them head over to where Matia is waiting without asking any more questions. I'm lucky to have such understanding classmates.

Without delaying any longer, I head inside the peristyle courts. I doubt Bebi and Minnefer are the extent of the operation, but at least catching them in the act is a start.

Chapter 15

Even Matia seems hesitant as I make my way up to the front door of the High Priest's house. I've never been here before, and wish I was arriving with Nik instead of on my own.

I knock firmly on the wooden door. There's no use putting off the inevitable. If I'm lucky, I'll still have a position at the temple once this conversation is over.

If I'm not...

I push the thought aside. Hori hadn't been impressed that we'd skipped the funeral, but he seemed relieved about us catching two of the people behind the organ stealing.

The door swings open revealing Nik on the other side of it. I sigh with relief. I haven't seen him since yesterday, and while I know it's irrational, I've been worrying about him ever since.

"Are you okay?" he asks.

"Nervous," I admit. "You?"

"I'm fine."

I raise an eyebrow, surprised to realise I can tell he's not telling me the whole truth.

"You should come in. Father is waiting for us."

"You don't call him dad?"

Nik shakes his head. "I used to, but when it became clear I'd be joining his priesthood, he suggested I start using father because it sounds more official."

"What it sounds like is exhausting," I mutter.

"Being the son of a High Priest is that," he agrees.

He leads me through the house. It doesn't look that much different from any other home I've been in, even if it's three times the size. There aren't even many ostentatious signs of wealth.

We come to a closed door which Nik knocks on.

"Come in," High Priest Ahmose calls.

Worry fills me over the conversation that's about to come.

"We're not going to be kicked out of the priest-hood, are we?" I ask.

"I honestly don't know. But I doubt it," he assures me. "I'm sure we can convince Father not to do that."

"I hope you're right." After hoping I'd get to serve Anubis for so long, I don't want to end up kicked out during my first year as an apprentice.

"Take a seat," the High Priest says, indicating to two chairs.

I hurry to the one on the left, with Nik taking the other one and Matia sitting between us looking rather pleased with herself. She probably should be. Her playful personality is what stopped Bebi from escaping, whereas all Nik and I did was hide in a fridge and get lucky.

"I think you know why the two of you are in my office today," the High Priest says.

We both nod.

"What you did was reckless. Not only could you have gotten yourselves seriously hurt, but you could also have ruined the vizier's funeral. Do you realise what kind of problems that could have caused? Not just for this temple, but for the Temple of Anubis around the entire world?"

"I'm sorry. We didn't intend to confront anyone, we just wanted to find proof so we could report the situation," I say.

High Priest Ahmose sighs. "I'm aware of your motivations, and they've been taken into account when it comes to your punishment. While I realise that you were both trying to act for the good of the temple, this recklessness can't go unpunished. You're both on clean-up duty for the next month. There'll be no embalming lessons in that time, and you'll have to stay late to do extra sanitising of the work-stations."

I let out a sigh of relief. That's not as bad as it could have been.

"What happened with Bebi and Minnefer?" Nik asks.

The High Priest raises an eyebrow, probably surprised that he's asked. I'm glad he has. I want to know what's happening with them too.

"Minnefer has confessed to everything. He'll be sent to the Halls of Ma'at for a trial at the end of the week. We don't think he has anything else to tell us. Bebi is proving harder to crack. Even with the evidence we have from the two of you and what Minnefer has admitted, he's refusing to talk."

"Do you think he will?" I ask.

"At this point, I don't know," the High Priest responds. "But if he doesn't, he'll also be sent for a trial. If Minnefer is found guilty, then I suspect he will be as well. The two of you will have to be witnesses at the trial, but we'll prepare you the best we can when the time comes."

Oh no, a trial sounds dramatic. I know I won't be the one at risk of being charged, but there's still something intimidating about knowing I'll have to go and sit in the Hall of Ma'at. The priests and priestesses who serve the goddess of justice as part of the legal system have a reputation for being fierce and unforgiving in their quest for the truth.

"Unfortunately, neither of them are revealing anything about who they work for," the High Priest says, breaking through my thoughts. "In both of your reports of the incident, you say that you examined several boxes of organs before hiding in the fridge."

"We did," Nik says quickly.

"There were some livers, a set of lungs, and a heart," I add.

The High Priest nods. "Do either of you know what happened to them?"

Nik shakes his head. "They were gone by the time we left the fridge. I assumed Bebi had taken them to whoever was waiting while we were in there."

"We don't even know who the heart belonged to," I admit.

"We've already started searches for the person the heart belongs to, but it's going to take some time. Hopefully, the family will be understanding if we offer them a better mummification treatment for their loved one, but we need to try and keep this as quiet as possible. If it comes out that we've been embalming people without hearts, then we're going to have a small scandal on our hands."

I grimace. That doesn't sound good. I try to keep the guilt under control. It isn't my fault this has been happening The only thing I've done is brought it to light. And that would probably have happened anyway.

"Sorry," Nik murmurs.

The High Priest sighs. "Regardless of how reckless you were, what you did has still helped people."

"I'm glad we could serve the temple," I respond, unsure about what else I can say.

"But next time you have suspicions like this, bring them to me. I don't want to hear more reports of you getting into unnecessarily dangerous situations," he says sternly, his gaze flitting between the two of us.

I smile weakly. "I'll do my best," I promise.

"Me too," Nik adds.

"Good. In which case, you're dismissed. I've already informed Hori of your punishment, expect your cleaning duties to start tomorrow."

"Thank you," I say as I get to my feet. "Come, Matia."

Nik takes a little longer to follow suit.

He follows me out of the building and into the late afternoon sunshine. I walk towards the lake and accidentally end up in fits of manic laughter.

"Are you okay?" he asks.

"I'm sorry," I say once I've regained some of my composure. "I've just been so stressed about that meeting."

A smile twists at Nik's lips. "I told you it'd be okay, even if we got into trouble."

"You did. You're a man of your word."

"I aim to be."

Matia rushes off in search of a stick before I can say anything to her. It seems that we're going to be enjoying some time outside.

"Do you want to stay and play fetch with us?" I ask Nik. "You don't have to run after the stick, I promise."

"That sounds good." He flashes me a genuine smile, which I return easily.

It's hard to believe he's gone from being insufferable to something like a friend.

Matia must sense that he's agreed to stay, as she decides to drop the stick by his feet. He leans down and scratches her head while he retrieves the stick and flings it easily over his head.

She leaps into action, making happy play sounds as she goes.

This is the kind of thing I can get used to, especially when I get to spend time with someone who feels as seriously about serving the temple as I do. For all his faults, Nik definitely wanted what's best for Anubis and the priesthood, and that's something I can respect.

Chapter 16

I brush the hair out of my eyes and lean on the mop I'm cleaning the floor with. "How long left until we're done with our punishment?" I ask.

"Two weeks and six days," Nik responds quickly.

I groan. "Why is it so long? We did a good thing, right?"

He chuckles. "You know we did. But this is a punishment for being reckless."

"Then I feel like you should have been a gentleman and taken on my portion too," I tease.

"Not happening."

"It was your idea to come into the mortuary and your sneeze that got us caught."

"That's fair. But I'm still not taking on an extra month of cleaning. If I have to suffer, you do too."

I grin widely, telling from the way he's talking that he's not too bothered by it. I think it helps that we're at the top of our class. No embalming for a few weeks isn't going to put us too behind. But hopefully, once we're done with this, we'll be allowed to deal with the bodies again. Sweeping up debris is getting tedious already.

We lapse into comfortable silence as we carry on our cleanup.

"Are you done with this?" Nik asks, gesturing to my mop bucket.

I nod.

"Want me to empty it for you?"

"If you like, but I can do it."

"It's no bother. We're a team, Ani. Teams help each other."

"I suppose we are, yes." And I like the sound of that, more than I would have thought a few months back.

"Good." He picks up the bucket and takes it over to one of the drains. He tips it up and pink-tinged water sloshes over the floor, disappearing forever.

I watch him out of the corner of my eye. I like working with him. Even if we're doing menial chores, there's something easy about being in the same room.

"What are you doing on your rest day tomorrow?" Nik asks as he returns from emptying the bucket.

I shrug. "I don't really have any plans. I normally spend it with my parents or my best friend. What about you?"

"I was thinking about going to one of the markets."

"Oh, with anyone?"

"No, I was wondering if..."

The door opens, cutting him off mid-sentence.

Footsteps sound, drawing our attention in the direction of the front door. To my surprise, Prince Ramesses steps into the mortuary. I hadn't even realised he was still here, I assumed he'd left after the vizier's funeral, completely forgetting that he'd told me otherwise when we first met.

"Ah, good, I was told I'd find you here," Ramesses says.

I start to turn my attention back to my chores, assuming he means Nik.

"What can we do for you?" Nik asks, clearly thinking the same thing.

"It's more what Ani can do," Ramesses responds. "I have a formal banquet tomorrow and I don't have a date, I was wondering if I could ask her to attend on my arm. It'll be a great opportunity for both of us."

"Oh." Surprise floods through me.

I glance at Nik, wondering what he thinks about the offer, and if he's going to finish asking me what I think he was trying to.

"It's just dinner," he promises. "Seven courses, but still just dinner."

"Okay, sure." I'm a little hesitant about it, but it's probably best not to reject him outright given who he is and the importance of his family.

"Great. I'll pick you up two hours before sundown. I look forward to it." He smiles, causing two dimples to form on his cheeks. "I'll let you get back to your work. Nikare." He nods curtly to Nik.

We both watch as he walks back the way he came. I don't know about Nik, but I'm a little taken aback by the turn of events.

"I guess you have plans tomorrow after all."

Am I imagining it, or is there a hint of disappointment in his voice? I don't dwell on it.

"Apparently. I'll admit to that not being what I expected when I came here this morning."

"Do you actually want to go with him?"

I shrug. "You don't say no to a member of the royal family."

"That doesn't answer the question."

"I'll tell you the day after tomorrow," I admit. "Mum will be pleased."

"From experience, that's not a good enough reason to do something," he says.

"No, it isn't."

But I don't know Ramesses. Maybe I'll have the best time I can possibly imagine. Or maybe I'll spend the whole night thinking that I'd rather be hanging out with Nik.

The only way to find out is to go tomorrow and see.

Thank you for reading *Apprentice Of The Dead*, I hope you enjoyed it. Ani will be back in book two of the series, *Initiate Of The Jackal:* https://books. authorlauragreenwood.co.uk/initiateofthejackal

You can download a bonus scene from Nik's point of view here: https://books.authorlauragreenwood. co.uk/1m60l9tjkd

Author Note

Thank you for reading *Apprentice Of The Dead*, I hope you enjoyed it! This is a little bit of an abridged author note - honestly, I think I could write one the same length as the book for this one!

If you've read any of my *Forgotten Gods Universe* books, or if you've been hanging around in my Facebook Reader Group, you probably already know that Egyptology is a passion of mine. I spend my free time researching, taking Egyptology diplomas, and reading non-fiction about Ancient Egypt and the culture - and it's not a new thing. It's one of the things that's fascinated me since I was a child and my Dad showed me *The Mummy* for the first time (I now have an Evie Funko Pop sat on my desk too!), and this was only made more intense by actually visiting Egypt when I was thirteen and seeing places like the Valley of the Kings, Karnak Temple, and the pyramids (also on my desk is a statue of Anubis Dad got me while we were there).

But this series has a bit of a twist - it's set in London and is based in an alternate timeline where the Egyptian Empire never fell. This produced quite a thought exercise for me in what I needed to advance and what I needed to keep more traditional. It also led me in a slightly different direction than I expected originally - books about death and the mortuary industry (the recommendations on my retailer of choice are a very strange mix of history, urban fantasy, Regency romance, writing books, and books about death and serial killers now). Just in case it interests you, I have included a bibliography on my website of books I read while researching this particular series (and Egyptology in general): https://www.authorlauragreenwood.co. uk/p/the-apprentice-of-anubis-bibliography.html

The embalming process described in the book is based on the current method of embalming used in the Western world and is part of how the world has developed. Traditional mummification like the Egyptians are well known for will be coming later in the series though!

If you want to keep up to date with new releases and other news, you can join my Facebook Reader Group or mailing list.

Stay safe & happy reading!

- Laura

Get A Free Apprentice Of Anubis Story

Is learning the art of mummification everything Dhara wants it to be?

After Dhara is chosen as one of the newest apprentices at the London Temple of Anubis, she's thrown into life at the temples, from learning about embalming, to the protective amulets used for the dead.

With the help of her mentor, she learns precisely what she needs in order to make it to ordination and to become a full Priestess Of Anubis.

Duty To The Dead is a standalone companion story to The Apprentice Of Anubis series, an urban fantasy set in an alternative version of London where the Egyptian Empire never fell. Duty To The Dead can be read as a standalone. The events take place during the events of Death Of The Pharaoh through to Court Of The Queen.

You can download Duty To The Dead for free here: https://books.authorlauragreenwood.co.uk/dhara

Also by Laura Greenwood

You can find out more about each of my series on my website.

- Obscure Academy: a paranormal romance series set at a university-age academy for mixed supernaturals. Each book follows a different couple.
- The Apprentice Of Anubis: an urban fantasy series set in an alternative world where the Ancient Egyptian Empire never fell. It follows a new apprentice to the temple of Anubis as she learns about her new role.
- Forgotten Gods: a paranormal adventure romance series inspired by Egyptian mythology. Each book follows a different Ancient Egyptian goddess.
- Amethyst's Wand Shop Mysteries (with Arizona Tape): an urban fantasy murder mystery series following a witch who teams up with a detective to solve murders. Each book includes a different murder.
- Grimm Academy: a fantasy fairy tale academy series. Each book follows a different fairy tale heroine.

- Jinx Paranormal Dating Agency: a paranormal romance series based on worldwide mythology where paranormals and deities take part in events organised by the Jinx Dating Agency. Each book follows a different couple.
- Purple Oasis (with Arizona Tape): a paranormal romance series based at a sanctuary set up after the apocalypse. Each book follows a different couple.
- Speed Dating With The Denizens Of The Underworld (shared world): a paranormal romance shared world based on mythology from around the world. Each book follows a different couple.
- Blackthorn Academy For Supernaturals (shared world): a paranormal monster romance shared world based at Blackthorn Academy. Each book follows a different couple.

You can find a complete list of all my books on my website:

https://books.authorlauragreenwood.co.uk/book-list

Signed Paperback & Merchandise:

You can find signed paperbacks, hardcovers, and merchandise based on my series (including stickers, magnets, face masks, and more!) via my website:

https://books.authorlauragreenwood.co.uk/shop

About Laura Greenwood

Laura is a USA Today Bestselling Author of paranormal romance, urban fantasy, and fantasy romance. When she's not writing, she drinks a lot of tea, tries to resist French macarons, and works towards a diploma in Egyptology. She lives in the UK, where most of her books are set. Laura specialises in quick reads, with healthy relationships and consent-positive moments regardless of if she's writing light-hearted romance, mythology-heavy urban fantasy, or anything in between.

Follow Laura Greenwood

- Website: www.authorlaura-greenwood.co.uk
- Mailing List: https://books.authorlauragreenwood.co.uk/newsletter
- Facebook Group: http://facebook.com/groups/theparanormalcouncil
- Facebook Page: http://facebook.com/authorlauragreenwood

- Bookbub: https://www.bookbub.com/authors/laura-greenwood